P9-DBI-061

Presentation

_____
For

_____
From

_____
Date

For God so loved the world that He gave His one and only Son,
that whoever believes in Him shall not perish but have eternal life.
For God did not send His Son into the world to condemn
the world, but to save the world through Him.

JOHN 3:16-17

Elsie's Christmas Party

How to Plan, Prepare and Host

An Old-Fashioned Christmas Party

793.22
ELS

Elsie's Christmas Party
Copyright © 2000, Mission City Press, Inc. All Rights Reserved.

Published by Mission City Press, Inc.

No part of this publication may be reproduced, stored in a retrieval system, or transmitted in any form or by any means — electronic, mechanical, photocopying, recording, or any other — without the prior written permission of the Publisher.

Cover Design: Richmond & Williams, Nashville, TN
Interior Design: Whisner Design Group, Tulsa, OK
Photography: Michelle Grisco Photography, West Covina, CA
                       Reg Francklyn Photography, Colorado Springs, CO
                       William Jackson Goff Photography, Nashville, TN
Decorating: Decorating on a Dime, Colorado Springs, CO
Food Prep & Design: Elaine Staff and Barbara York, Nashville, TN
Typesetting: BookSetters, White House, TN
Text: Candy Paull, Nashville, TN

Unless otherwise indicated, all Scripture references are from the Holy Bible, New International Version (NIV). Copyright ©1973, 1978, 1984 by International Bible Society. Used by permission of Zondervan Publishing House, Grand Rapids, MI. All rights reserved.

Elsie Dinsmore and Elsie Dinsmore: A Life of Faith are trademarks of Mission City Press, Inc.

For more information, write to Mission City Press at P.O. Box 681913, Franklin, Tennessee 37068-1913, or visit our Web Site at:

www.elsie–dinsmore.com

ISBN #: 1-928749-52-6
Library of Congress Card Number: 00-191557

Printed in the United States of America
1 2 3 4 5 6 7 8 — 06 05 04 03 02 01 00

1999

TABLE OF CONTENTS

The youngest children caught it first. Then it spread to the older children, the servants, and the guests. Finally even the elder Mr. Dinsmore was infected. "It" was the spirit of Christmas Eve at Roselands.

All day long, the heavy doors into the parlor had been tightly shut. Only a few were allowed entrance — Mrs. Dinsmore, Adelaide, Pompey, and two others of the house servants. Time and again, they were seen going into the room, carrying mysterious boxes and bundles. Elsie, Carrie, and the older children knew what was happening, of course, but they all — even Arthur Dinsmore, who was usually the first to spoil a surprise — kept their silence around the little ones.

When supper in the playroom was over that evening, the children began to wander downstairs to the drawing room where their parents and the other guests were gathered. The drawing room was brightly lit with an abundance of candles, but brighter still was the sense of anticipation that hummed throughout the room. As the clock approached eight, everyone began to assemble — as if by some common order — in the entry hall outside the parlor. All conversation died down to no more than a soft whisper, and all eyes were soon directed to the portal behind which something exciting lay.

Suddenly, the parlor doors opened, seemingly of their own accord. The long room beyond was dim and apparently empty, save for a dazzling light at its far end, and the watchers gasped in astonishment. A thick pine tree, as tall as the room itself, was covered with hundreds of lighted tapers that glowed and twinkled like the night stars. As the servants rushed to light the sconces around the parlor walls, it became apparent that the tree was hung with countless small toys and colorfully wrapped presents tied to the pine branches with red and gold ribbons. Larger packages were arranged under the tree's lowest boughs. When this brilliant sight had sunk in a bit, old Mr. Dinsmore signaled for everyone to enter the room.

From *Elsie's Impossible Choice*,
Book Two of the *Elsie Dinsmore: A Life of Faith* Series

Introduction

Welcome to Elsie's Christmas Party

This book will give you a
glimpse of what Christmas was like
in Elsie Dinsmore's day, the Victorian era,
and give you ideas for bringing old-fashioned charm
into your life this Christmas. We hope that in these joyful
revels, you'll learn sweet lessons of friendship and caring. But
more than that, we hope you will succeed in hosting a memorable
event that allows everyone who attends to celebrate the Savior of
mankind, Jesus Christ, and to more fully enjoy
the real meaning of Christmas.

May this book bless you and bring you many happy hours of
fun, friendship and creativity.

Meet Elsie Dinsmore

Elsie Dinsmore came into being in 1868 when author Martha Finley (1828-1909) brought her to life through a series of fiction books called "The Elsie Books." Set in the American South in the mid-to-late 1800s, the books tell the captivating story of the life and spiritual commitment of Elsie Dinsmore, a charming young heroine whose unshakable Christian faith guides her through the joys, trials and adventures of childhood, adolescence, young adulthood, marriage, and motherhood.

Although Elsie Dinsmore is a fictional character who grows up in a different era, there is something about her that makes girls of all ages want to be like her— so full of inner peace, joy and strength, (no matter how difficult the circumstances), so loving and kind, so gentle in heart and spirit, and so devoted to God. Elsie is a nineteenth century girl with the power to inspire and uplift people of any era.

Now, almost a century after Miss Finley's death, Elsie's stories are being introduced to a whole new generation of girls. The original nineteenth century text has been carefully revised, updated and enhanced for contemporary readers.

Although set in a distant time (nearly two decades before the American Civil War), Elsie's adventures are now as lively, engaging, and relevant as the best of modern fiction. Through exciting stories centered on the Word of God, you can take a trip back in time and share Elsie's struggles, her hopes and dreams, and her unwavering faith. Once you know this extraordinary character, you will find it hard to forget her.

The first four books in the
Elsie Dinsmore: A Life of Faith Series

Martha Finley

Martha Finley was born in 1828 in Chillicothe, Ohio, the daughter of a busy doctor with a large family. Martha's mother died when she was young, but her devout stepmother encouraged and nurtured Martha's gift for writing. Well-educated for a girl of her times, Martha eventually became a teacher. Three years after she began writing *Elsie Dinsmore*, the story of the lonely little Southern girl was accepted by a New York publisher. The book became an instant bestseller in 1868, eventually expanding to twenty-eight volumes. For almost forty years, legions of dedicated readers eagerly welcomed each new Elsie book. The series was the best-selling juvenile fiction of its day, enjoyed by an estimated twenty-five million readers! Martha Finley died in 1909 just before her eighty-second birthday. She never married, but left behind a beautiful legacy of faith through the *Elsie Dinsmore* series.

Part One

Christmas in Elsie's Time

When we think
of Christmas celebrations,
we think of manger scenes, church services,
Christmas carols, giving to others, family parties, tables full
of food, Christmas lights and ornaments, garland and greenery,
and the spread of brotherhood, kindness, and charity among all
people. But what was the celebration of Christmas like
in Elsie Dinsmore's era?

Was it the same as our celebrations today?

Elsie's Era

Elsie Dinsmore grew up in an era when entertaining others was truly an art. From creating an atmosphere of welcome to making sure each guest had a delightful time, a hostess in Elsie's day was a living example of grace, charm and Christ-like love in action.

When we first meet Elsie Dinsmore, she is living on her grandfather's plantation, known as Roselands, in the southern United States in the 1840s, right in the middle of the nineteenth century. It was a time that was also known as the "Victorian" era. The Victorian era took its name from the reign of the English Queen, Victoria. She ruled from 1837 to 1901.

Queen Victoria

"I will be good," a little girl of twelve said when told she would one day be queen of the British Empire. Victoria was eighteen when she became Queen of England in 1837, and she reigned for sixty-four years until her death in 1901. As a young girl, Victoria spent a sheltered childhood at Kensington Palace with her mother and her governess. She read the Bible, as well as sermons and religious tracts, and became a symbol of respectability and family life, giving her name to an extraordinary era. When she married German Prince Albert of Saxe-Coburg, it was a true love match that the world would admire and imitate.

Christmas in the Nineteenth Century

When the nineteenth century first began, Christmas was a very different holiday than the Christmas we know today. At that time, the celebration of Christmas was largely in decline. In many places, Christmas was just another workday. In others, Christmas celebrations were actually banned. Though many individuals celebrated Christmas to various degrees, it was not until the Victorian era that the celebration of Christmas began to be revived in a widespread way, and Christmas as we know it became a permanent and important part of our culture.

It was in the mid-to-late nineteenth

century that Christmas trees became popular, the Santa Claus legend emerged, Christmas carols were revitalized, commercial ornaments were first developed, stores began advertising to Christmas shoppers, and the celebration of Christmas Day became a public holiday in the United States.

Although by the mid–1800s, many elements of our modern Christmas had come into existence, for most of the nineteenth century, Christmas was still a small, family celebration with simple homemade gifts. It wasn't until the dawning of the twentieth century that Christmas became much more elaborate—from the availability of elegant glass ornaments to more sophisticated choices in Christmas shopping and entertainment.

People Who Influenced Christmas

Several people from the nineteenth century greatly influenced the development of Christmas celebrations as we know them today. One was British author Charles Dickens. His stories, especially *A Christmas Carol* of 1843, rekindled the joy of Christmas in England and America in a significant way. The impact of *A Christmas Carol*, which told the story of the reform of the hard-hearted, Christmas-hating Ebenezer Scrooge, painted an unforgettable picture of Christmas that is considered a classic today.

The great popularity of Queen Victoria and Prince Albert also did much to revive and develop many Christmas traditions in Victorian time. In 1850, *Godey's Lady's Book* magazine published a picture of Queen Victoria and her husband and children celebrating around the Christmas tree. Prince Albert had brought many customs to England from his homeland of Germany, including the Christmas tree, which had been part of German tradition since the seventeenth century. The magazine picture did

much to encourage the use of Christmas trees in America. A "German tree" was even part of the White House Christmas of President Franklin Pierce in 1856. In addition, because the much-admired royal family emphasized the importance of Christmas not only as a religious holiday, but as a time for friends and family as well, Christmas celebrations in the nineteenth century became more family-oriented than ever before.

Two writers from New York also greatly affected how people thought about the season and helped create the familiar images of a Victorian Christmas. First, Washington Irving wrote a series of stories called *Bracebridge Hall* about a fictional English manor house that celebrated Christmas with feasting and acts of kindness to people of the lower classes. Then Clement Clarke Moore, a friend of Washington Irving, wrote the popular poem called "The Night Before Christmas" in 1822. As a result, Santa Clauses began to appear on street corners and in stores by the 1850s.

Santa Claus

Santa Claus is a tradition that developed in the nineteenth century. Nicholas of

Myra was a fourth century pastor who became famous for his charitable work on behalf of the poor, the despised, and the rejected. Long after his death, the stories of this popular man continued, and eventually he grew to be known as "Father Christmas" who gave gifts to good children on December 6th, Saint Nicholas' Day.

His Dutch name was pronounced "Sinterklaas." The Germans had "Christ Kindel" (meaning a young messenger of Christ), later evolving into Kris Kringle. They also had pagan elves that would appear driving a sled pulled by Cracker and Gnasher. All these different cultural traditions were brought to America by immigrants, and in the melting pot of ideas the legend of Santa Claus and his eight reindeer was born.

When Clement Clarke Moore, an American minister living in New York, wrote *A Visit from Saint Nicholas*, also known as *The Night Before Christmas*, he transformed St. Nicholas into the familiar image of a the jolly old elf in his poem. When the poem appeared in *Harper's Weekly* in 1863 with illustrations by Thomas Nast, the drawings showed a fat jolly old man with a white beard and a red suit. In 1931, the Coca-Cola Company commissioned artist Haddon Sundblom to paint Santa

Claus for a Coca-Cola ad. He made Santa Claus into the larger-than-life cultural icon we know today.

A Southern Christmas

Christmas in the pre-Civil War South was the height of the social season. It was a time of lavish hospitality, brightly-lit plantation mansions, and endless rounds of visiting and entertaining. A tutor at a large Virginia plantation wrote in his diary, "Nothing is now to be heard of in conversation but the Balls, the Fox-Hunts, the fine entertainments, and the good fellowship, which are to be exhibited at the approaching Christmas."

It was three southern states (Alabama, Louisiana, and Arkansas) that were the first three states to declare Christmas a legal holiday. Betwen 1850 and 1861, fifteen other states followed suit. This legislation led to standardizing December 25 as the day Christmas is observed.

The Antebellum South

Antebellum means "before the war." Whenever people talk about the antebellum South, they are talking about life before the Civil War. The picture of a white-columned mansion, wide green lawns, magnolias and moonlight, elegant rooms full of antique furniture, and Southern belles fanning themselves on the porch, has become part of the mythology of the antebellum South.

But only a minority of Southerners lived in elegant mansions such as the ones Elsie and her

family owned. One-third of the people living in the South were slaves and another large group of people were poor farmers trying to compete with wealthy plantation owners. In the 1840s in America, slavery was, sadly, an accepted economic and social reality in the South, and the American Civil War (also known as the "War Between the States") was still two decades away. The plantation economy depended on slavery, but it also caused suffering for the poor whites who had to compete with the "free" labor of the slaves. It was a glorious time for a privileged few, but not for most ordinary people.

The end of the antebellum era came when the War Between the States began in December of 1860. South Carolina seceded from the United States and ten other southern states followed. The war was not only about slavery, but about states' rights as well.

After the South lost the war, many Southerners looked back to the pre-war years as a golden age. The antebellum South is now romanticized with images of ladies in hoopskirts, gallant soldiers, and ancestral homes that survived the war. But the reality was a tragic tale of great personal and national loss.

Today you can get a taste of what life was like back then. In the Nashville, Tennessee area, you can visit and tour the Carter House, the oldest, still-standing, battle-scarred structure of the Civil War, and Belle Meade Plantation, an elegant antebellum mansion with seven other historical buildings on the grounds. Many other modern Southern cities, like Natchez, Mississippi, offer spring and fall pilgrimages where old family homes are opened to the public and guides

dress in historical costumes.

Christmas on the Plantation

Christmas on the plantation was a busy season. Because travel was difficult, visitors would come to stay for days or even weeks at a time. Southern hospitality was legendary and lavish in plantation days.

Preparation would begin weeks in advance. Plans were made to feed and entertain many visitors throughout the holiday season. It took a lot of work to entertain on such an extravagant scale. For instance, Belle Meade Plantation employed over 100 servants and "hands" for the farm and housework. The farm and kitchen were kept busy feeding a constant stream of social and business guests.

On one plantation, the Christmas Day ritual included church services, gift opening, and an early afternoon dinner that allowed the servants to go home to their own celebrations. In the *Elsie Dinsmore* books, we see brief glimpses of Christmas on the plantations. At the Roselands Plantation, Christmas Eve celebrations began after supper with a tree and gift exchange. At The Oaks Plantation, Elsie and her father celebrated Christmas Day more quietly, with morning worship, distribution of gifts to the field and house slaves, a leisurely Christmas dinner, and a family gift exchange in the afternoon.

Christmas in the Slave Quarters

Throughout the antebellum period, most slaves lived on large farms and small plantations. Only a quarter of the slave population lived on plantations with more than fifty slaves. Masters were often cruel and treated their slaves very harshly. Although some owners prided themselves on caring for "their people," Bible readings, nursing the sick, and providing a minimum of comfort were no substitute for freedom. In spite of the inequalities, however, some families and their slaves grew greatly attached to each other.

The slaves usually lived in small cabins away from the main house. The house slaves were a step higher on the social ladder than the field hands. Christmas was a busy time for the house slaves, keeping up with the needs of visitors, guests, and the master's

family during the holiday festivities. And though field hands worked longer hours during the growing season, they still had to do a great deal of work to maintain the plantation during the holidays.

Sometimes the slaves were given a small Christmas celebration of their own and a brief respite from labor. A Christmas tree decorated with fruit and nuts or treats might be provided, and house slaves and servants might have received personal tokens or gifts from members of the family.

Letter Writing and Christmas Cards

Letter writing was an art in Victorian times. There were no computers, typewriters, or e-mails. Victorians took pride in their ability to write letters and develop friendships over long distances. Many courtships took place via the mail. Letters were treasured and read over and over. Elsie and many of her friends kept their friendship alive through writing letters.

Penmanship was very important. Victorians wrote with pens that could leave

blots on the paper if not carefully used. A lady was judged by her handwriting and a blotted page indicated carelessness. That was why Elsie worked so hard to avoid blotting her copybook. A slip of the hand and suddenly a carefully written word could have an unsightly black spot of ink marring its perfection.

Sending commercial Christmas cards to friends began in 1843 in England. Two early designers were J.C. Horsley and William Egley. The first commercial American cards were produced by Louis Prang, a German-born printer, in 1875. Prang awarded cash prizes for greeting card designs and helped many artists get their start in life. Prang also introduced art education into public schools, believing that children should be taught to appreciate fine art. His cards are collector's items, with work that is exquisite even by today's standards. Less expensive Christmas postcards became popular at the turn of the century, and by 1906 Christmas cards were considered an essential part of celebrating the season.

The Victorian Christmas Tree

The story of the decorated tree in America begins in Pennsylvania Dutch country. German settlers brought the custom of a Christmas tree with them when they immigrated to the United States. By the 1820s the trees were common in Pennsylvania. Everything was handmade, reflecting the resourceful spirit of people who lived close to the land. They would carve wooden stars and angels, bake cookies in the shapes of animals to hang on the tree, and string dried apples, nuts, and popcorn to garland the branches. Underneath the tree might be a manger scene or a gingerbread house along with wrapped gifts. On Christmas Eve children left straw baskets with hay in them. The hay was for the mule of the *Christkind*, or Christ child,

who they believed would go from home to home while the children were sleeping. Gifts called *Christkindles* would be left behind for the children to find on Christmas morning.

The kind of tree Elsie enjoyed had ornaments that were mostly handmade and often edible–cookies, candy, apples, nuts, and sweet-filled paper cornucopias. Many decorations were put together from lace and fabric scraps or odds and ends found around the house or yard. It wasn't until later in the century, in the 1870s, that simple glass balls and "store bought" ornaments made their appearance.

Christmas trees didn't have electric lights in Elsie's time— they had candles. As dangerous as it was, small candles would be wired to the branches of the tree (in places where the area above the candle was clear). The candles were lit only once, normally just moments before the children would enter the room. When the parlor doors opened, the children would behold the wonder of the lit tree for the first time; after a few moments of delight, the candles would be immediately extinguished. Electric lights didn't appear until 1910 and were very expensive. It wasn't until the 1920s and 1930s that electric lights were mass produced and thus affordable for most people.

Christmas Greens and Garlands

Victorians might not have had fancy store-bought decorations, but they used evergreens, ivy, boxwood, laurel, and other greens to garland doorways, mantles, staircases, and even framed pictures. Flowers, such as holly berries, poinsettias, chrysanthemums, and geraniums, enlivened the greenery.

The Poinsettia and the Pineapple

The poinsettia is a southern contribution to Christmas. The plant is named for U.S. Ambassador Joel Roberts Poinsett, who brought the plant back from Mexico to his hometown in South Carolina in the 1820s. It soon became popular because of its spectacular red blooms, perfect for the Christmas season.

The pineapple is a symbol of traditional Southern hospitality. It was used as decoration during Christmas time and year-round, whether it was as a fruit centerpiece or carved in wood on top of a bedpost or over a doorway. Victorian doorways were often decorated with a fan of apples topped with a pineapple.

Food Before Microwave Ovens and Refrigerators

Victorians loved to eat. But when Elsie was growing up, they did not have refrigerators and microwave ovens. The plantation might have a spring house, a cool cellar to store perishable food, or an icebox that literally had blocks of ice to keep food cold. In the warm South, ice was an expensive luxury, often shipped from northern ports in New England, where cutting and storing winter ice for summer use was big business. Much of the food eaten was fresh and in season, but limited to what could be grown on the plantation and in that climate. Winter meant more root vegetables and salted meats, while summer brought a profusion of fresh fruits and vegetables. Some luxuries, such as oranges, could survive shipment from other areas of the world. But most of the food eaten on the plantation was grown and processed right there, with only a few staples from the grocery store.

The wood stove had to be stoked with fuel and work in the kitchens was very hot. Sometimes the plantation kitchen was in a building separate from the big house. The servants would bring the food to the table down a breezeway or walkway. Feeding people took a great deal of effort and planning. It was a year-round job—from planting crops to butchering hogs — and everyone worked hard to put meals on the table.

Victorian Formal Table Settings

The Victorians loved to dine and entertain. And they loved to create an elegant table.

Smiley's Cook Book and New and Complete Guide for Housekeepers, printed in 1898, advised Victorian hostesses that "there is more art than many people imagine in setting a table properly. The table cloth should be laid evenly, with an equal amount falling over the two ends and sides....Nothing but the best white table cloths or napkins should be used for the dinner table....The object of a dinner party is not to make a display of fine table furniture or too elaborate cookery, but to promote agreeable social exchange and conversation among friends."

The Victorians used a mind-boggling array of spoons, forks, knives, cutlery, ladles, and servers—not to mention finger bowls. Different spoons were used for berries, coffee, dessert, soup, salt, sorbet, and tea, different forks for meat, pie, pastry, salad, and oysters, and different knives for butter, cheese, fish, jelly, pie, and waffles. How did young girls ever learn to keep them all straight?!

There were etiquette books and household manuals to prepare the Victorian woman for any question of manners. These books could tell readers the difference between a juice glass and a water goblet, and just where and when they should be placed on the table. They helped readers make sense of all that silverware and which fork should be used for an appetizer and which should be used for the main course. Good manners, such as knowing which fork to use, not only indicated social status, but also consideration for the hostess. And just in case you couldn't remember which fork to use when you were sitting at a formal dinner, you could watch your hostess and see which fork she was using!

Etiquette for a Proper Young Lady

Victorian children lived with many more rules and restrictions than we do today. They were treated as small adults and expected to behave accordingly. At mealtimes children were expected to have impeccable manners. They learned strict rules of behavior, were instructed not to be rough or rude, and followed rigid routines.

Adults were all-powerful, always to be obeyed, and never to be questioned. When children were in adult company, they were often dressed up and on their best behavior. They might be asked to sing or recite poetry or play a piano piece when visitors came.

Cleanliness, washing, hair brushing, and neatness of dress were essential. There was to be no chattering, especially at mealtimes and bedtime. There were limits on what could be eaten and how much. Restrictions and regulations were thought to build character in children.

Growing into adulthood was no easier. Though nursery rules might not be enforced any more, a young woman's entry into the world of adults was hedged about with dozens of do's and don'ts. When a young girl was allowed to put her hair up instead of wearing it down, she knew she was entering an adult world with adult responsibilities. Victorians were more formal than we are today, but good manners are always timeless when they show respect and kindness for others.

White Lace and Tartan Sashes

In September of 1842, Queen Victoria and her husband made their first trip to

Scotland. They fell in love with the land and in 1848 purchased *Balmoral*, a castle in Scotland. Through the years Victoria and Albert would visit Balmoral and find refreshment there, away from the crowds and demands of governing an empire. Because her subjects were fascinated with the Queen's life, interest in all things Scottish grew more popular as the royal family's ties with Scotland deepened.

Tartans, clans, Scottish folklore, the poet Robert Burns, and the Victorian novels of Sir Walter Scott seized the romantic imagination of the world. Its biggest fans were Victoria and Albert, and they decorated Balmoral with the Balmoral tartan. America also fell in love with Scottish styles and there was a rage for tartan plaid and Robert Burns in mid-century. Many Scots immigrated to America, bringing their heritage with them. That is why even today, one of the prettiest ways to celebrate Christmas with a Scottish air is to use tartan as an accent for clothing and decoration. Whether it was by tying a tartan bow on a green wreath, or wearing a pretty tartan sash on a white lace dress, or dressing up in a red tartan skirt, Victorian ladies and

girls loved tartan at Christmas.

Old-Fashioned Parlor Pastimes

Victorians loved games. Outside they played lawn games, such as croquet and badminton. Inside, parlor games offered entertainment for everyone. The games most enjoyed were a happy combination of amusement and companionship.

Word games and skits were especially popular in Victorian times. Charades used short theatricals or pantomimes to guess words or phrases. A pile of old clothes, hats, shawls, and other props inspired the dramatists to enact words like friendship, moonstruck, sweetmeat, and toadstool. Sometimes the charade would enact a saying, such as "the early bird gets the worm."

"Tableaux Vivants" were expensively costumed and staged motionless scenes of one or more people representing favorite subjects from Shakespeare, historic events, nursery rhymes, famous paintings, fairy tales and Bible stories.

An evening of parlor games would often include a silly game that made sure everyone made some kind of mistake. They would be penalized and forfeit something that they would have to redeem with clever absurdities or some form of ridiculous behavior designed to inspire hearty laughter.

❧

Magic Lantern Shows: The Victorian "Movie"

Victorians had no movie theaters or televisions in their homes. But they did have access to an entertainment technology that would lay the groundwork for the modern movie. It was called a "magic lantern show." The first projector was invented in the 1650s. By the late 1700s and early 1800s, wandering showmen traveled around, putting on small scale shows using a lantern lit with a single candle. Programs would be shown with glass slides illuminated by bright lights onto a full-size screen. By the end of the nineteenth century, magic lantern shows used limelight to project hand-colored slides. Limelight produced a light as powerful as a modern movie projector and shows were created that filled theaters across the nation. A live showman and a musician told the story and provided dramatic sound effects. The audience participated with cheers, boos, applause, and responses to the showman's directions. It offered a memorable night of entertainment for all ages.

In the nineteenth century, magic lantern shows were a regular part of public and home entertainment. They used visual storytelling techniques that were adapted in the new nickelodeon and film industry at the beginning of the twentieth century. Motion pictures soon eclipsed the magic lantern shows and ended their long run of popularity with the public.

Christmas Carols and Hymns

Christmas carols are an important part of celebrating the season. The word "carol" comes from an old French word, carole, meaning to dance in a ring. Singing carols door-to-door started with the Anglo-Saxon custom of wassailing, which means to bless with good health. Farm families would bless the trees for the next year's growing season by walking around the orchard. They sang as they walked and ended the ceremony with wassail, an apple drink.

Medieval Christmas music followed the

Gregorian tradition, which was based on the monks' and nuns' chanting of the liturgy of the church. In Renaissance Italy, a lighter and more joyous Christmas song emerged, more like the spirit of the carols we know today.

Caroling fell out of fashion for awhile. Some of the Puritans even banned carols because they were considered frivolous music. Hymns were allowed, but carols had a "wild" history of belonging more to folk festivals than church traditions.

During the Victorian era, carols were reclaimed for the Christmas celebrations and new ones were written to honor Christ's birth. Music by Handel and Mendelssohn was adapted for these songs. Perhaps the most famous of all Christmas carols, "Silent Night", was written by Franz Gruber in 1818.

Gifts and the Spirit of Giving

Exchanging gifts during this special time of year has always been an important feature of Christmas celebrations. It is a reminder that it is more blessed to give than to receive and that God loves a cheerful giver (Acts 20:35; 2 Cor. 9:7). Originally an act of covenant and renewal, gift giving is meant to be a reminder of

the greatest Gift of all, when God sent His Son Jesus to save the world.

Elsie grew up in a tradition of giving and generosity. Victorian Christians believed that charity and good works were an important expression of their faith. Giving without thought of return was the ideal for which they strove.

Not what we give, but what we share—
For the gift without the giver is bare.
Who gives himself with his alms
     feeds three—
Himself, his hungering neighbor, and Me.
James Russell Lowell (1819-1891)

Handmade with Love

Under a Victorian Christmas tree, you might see some of the same types of items you see today, like dolls, toys, train sets, picture books, games, jewelry, and clothes. But most of the gifts given in the era when Elsie was growing up were hand-made. The best gifts required more time than money. Women's magazines encouraged everyone to make gifts. Embroidery, beadwork, needlepoint, and lacework offered ways to create one-of-a-kind gifts out of the sewing box. Sachets, needle books, aprons, purses, fans, slippers, pin cushions, pen wipers, pillow covers, waistcoats, handkerchiefs, collars, and fans were made out of scraps of cotton, silk, lace, and linen. An editor wrote in 1890, *"An article that one makes is certainly a more complimentary gift than one bought, for we weave with every stitch sweet wishes for the recipient that untold gold cannot purchase."*

Gifts for the Poor and for Missions

It has always been a tradition that Christians give generously. Victorian Christians felt that

giving to missions and taking care of the poor, needy, sick, and despised in society was just as important as going to church on Sunday. Real faith showed itself in good deeds as well as right beliefs.

Stories like Charles Dickens' *A Christmas Carol* asserted that brotherhood, kindness, and charity should be a part of life, and that Christmas was a natural season for giving generously. True giving from the heart helps Christmas become

more real and more meaningful to us all.

One ancient legend says that the Christ Child wanders the earth on Christmas Eve, disguised as a beggar seeking shelter and food. An act of mercy or kindness can be a symbolic gesture of love for Jesus. "As you did it to one of the least of these, my children, you did it to me," says Matthew 25.

Somehow not only for Christmas
But all the long year through,
The joy that you give to others
Is the joy that comes back to you.
And the more you spend in blessing
The poor and lonely and sad,
The more of your heart's possessing
Returns to make you glad.
John Greenleaf Whittier (1807-1892)

Part Two
Your Old-Fashioned Christmas Party

You can host a
Christmas party in the Victorian spirit of fun
and good fellowship. You're probably used to informal
parties with pizza and soft drinks and chips. But Elsie's entertainments
were much more formal. You can have fun with party planning,
creating an elegant table, decorating a beautiful tree, preparing delicious
foods, dressing up in something beautiful, enjoying parlor games and
sharing the Christmas story.

In the following pages you'll find a variety of ideas for planning,
preparing and hosting your own old-fashioned
Christmas party. Enjoy!

What Matters Most

*C*hristmas is a wonderful time of the year. But it is all too easy to lose sight of the reason for the season in the midst of the excitement, the busy preparations, and the noise of commercialism. Yes, it is a time for gift-giving, family togetherness, making memories and strengthening friendships. But if there is one thing to remember during the Christmas holiday season, it is that *the true meaning of Christmas has to do with God's enormous love both for you as an individual and for all of mankind.*

Elsie Dinsmore understood this, and her simple faith can be a stirring example to modern girls. Elsie may not have ridden in a plane or a car or played video games or used a computer, but she knew the timeless secret of Christmas: that God loved her so much that He sent His own beloved Son Jesus to earth as a man so that He could die for her and bear the punishment for her sins and for the sins of all people everywhere.

In doing this, God was giving us all a free gift— the gift of forgiveness of our sins and an eternal relationship with Him. It is a gift that no one could ever earn or buy. And though it cost God a great price, the death of His dear Son, for us it is really and truly free. All we have to do is accept the gift. *"For God so loved the world that He gave His one and only Son, that whoever believes in Him shall not perish but have eternal life. For God did not send His Son into the world to condemn the world, but to save the world through Him."* JOHN 3:16-17

As you prepare for your party, remember the baby born in Bethlehem who grew up and later gave His life so that you could be reconciled to God, our Heavenly Father. Take some time out to meditate on the Scriptures that tell about Jesus' birth in Luke, chapters 1 and 2, or Matthew, chapters 1 and 2.

If you haven't done so already, accept the free gift of God— the gift of Jesus— and rejoice this season in the real meaning of Christmas.

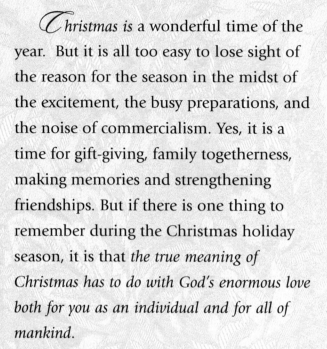

Planning Your Party

Now that you have learned what Christmas was like in the nineteenth century when Elsie Dinsmore was growing up, it is time to plan your own old-fashioned Christmas party. It will probably be a little more formal than the typical party, and it may take some extra work, but it will be a rewarding way to bless your friends and loved ones and give you a taste of what life was like in the past.

The first step, and one of the most important, is coming up with a plan for your party. A good hostess will care about even the smallest details of her party, and to ensure a success, you need to plan ahead. The time you spend making lists and determining every aspect of the party in advance will ensure that you, the hostess, are relaxed and ready to enjoy the party along with your guests. You might even want to ask two or three friends to help you plan.

As you begin to think about your party, you should take some notes on a separate piece of paper. The specific details and plans for each aspect of your party will take shape over time as you consider and choose from a variety of options. However, it is a good idea to begin writing down ideas and questions and keeping written lists from the very outset. Here are some examples of things you might want to write down as you plan your party:

- *the names and addresses of guests you would like to invite*

- *what the color theme will be*

- *the best date and time options for your party*

- *what decorations you want for your tree, table and room, and what decorating supplies you will need*

- *what dishes, silverware, and table linens you will use*

- *what your menu will be and what groceries you will need*

- *what entertainment, if any, you want at your party*

- *etc.*

Choosing a Color Theme

Decorating for your party around a color theme will help you coordinate all aspects of the party and give your guests a sense of being surrounded by a certain look and feel. When people think of Christmas, they usually think of red and green, but there are many colors and choices. You have probably seen modern Christmas displays with color themes other than red and green, such as purple and gold, all white, all peach, etc. So feel free to be creative!

Two very Victorian color themes that you might consider for your Christmas party are pink and white (a feminine look which can make use of lots of pretty lace, ribbon and flowers), or a red and green tartan plaid (a more traditional Christmas look).

Whatever color theme you choose, ideally you should try to incorporate those colors into as many aspects of your party as possible.

Simple Yet Elegant

Elegance does not have to be expensive. Although some Victorians, such as the Dinsmore family, had a good deal of wealth and could afford to buy costly items for use in entertaining others, the average person in Victorian times used simple, inexpensive, readily available items. Ordinary things, such as flowers, greenery, fabric scraps, fruit, and candles, can be blended together to create an elegant and elaborate look.

Invitations

Party invitations in Elsie's day would have taken the form of a personal, handwritten letter or note. Elsie probably would have used a fancy quill pen that she dipped into a well of ink. Most likely, Elsie would have also used each letter as an opportunity to add other personal comments specific to each recipient, since they did not have telephones or e-mail to catch up with each other in Elsie's day. So every one of Elsie's invitation letters would probably have been unique to the person, as opposed to the more "mass-produced" kind of invitation, which has the same message for each person. Feel free to write yours either way.

Whatever form it takes, your invitation should be handwritten in your very best penmanship, and preferably handmade in other respects too. It can either be a personal letter on pretty stationery, or something creative made with ribbons, buttons, etc. Even a postcard can be dressed up for Christmas. Remember to invite people well ahead of time. Because Christmas is a busy time and people's calendars tend to fill up fast, deliver your invitations at least three to four weeks in advance of your party. You may deliver them by mail, or by personally handing them to each person.

Remember to invite enough people for good cheer, but not so many that it will be crowded or hard to manage. And invite guests who will blend well together. Be sure to keep a written list of the guests you are inviting. On your list, record the dates you send or deliver the invitations and each person's reply.

Homemade Invitations

Items Needed:

- ☐ A single hole punch
- ☐ Red and green thin ribbon – 1/8" wide
- ☐ Red and green tartan ribbon – 1/2" wide
- ☐ Buttons in a color that coordinates with your ribbon
- ☐ Glue stick or white glue
- ☐ Calligraphy pen – black or gold or another color
- ☐ Blank cards
- ☐ Envelopes to match the color and size of the cards
- ☐ Stamps and Scissors

Instructions:

1. Fold the card in half and on the inside lower half of the card, write the information about your party, being careful to start your first line at least 1 full inch or more below the fold of the card.

2. Make sure your invitation includes: your name, the date, time and location of the party (and a map, if necessary), and any special instructions. Also, it is helpful to let people know if a meal will be served and what type of clothing you would like them to wear. If you are having a formal party, you might not want people to show up in jeans or shorts. Likewise, if you are having a casual party, you might not want them to show up in their dressiest clothes. "Holiday attire" will tell people that they should wear festive clothes. You might even want to be more specific, such as "wear red and green colors." And you may want to put "R.S.V.P." (French for *repondez s'il vous plait* meaning "Reply, if you please"). When you add "R.S.V.P." to an invitation, you are politely asking your guests to let you know if they will be able to attend. It's a small courtesy, but it really does help to know when you're planning a party. If you don't get replies, call people and find out if they are planning to come.

3. Fold your card in half and punch two small holes at the top center of the card at least 3/8" below the fold, leaving at least 1/4" of space in between the holes.

4. Cut a strip of tartan ribbon to the exact width of your card and glue it on the card horizontally, right underneath the two holes.

5. Cut two strips of equal length of your red and green thin ribbons. Hold them together and thread both ends of the two ribbons through the two holes in your card, going from back to front. Tie them in a bow at the front of the card.

6. At the center just under the bow, glue the button.

7. Use a calligraphy pen to write the message on the front of the card. If you have never used one before, don't worry. Just have some fun practicing writing with it. Even if you don't become skilled at calligraphy, it will still give your handwriting an elegant touch.

A Note About How To Treat Your Guests

As the hostess, you want everyone to have a good time at your party. Be dressed and ready in plenty of time. If there are many last minute preparations, you might want to ask a friend to come early and give you a hand. You'll be more relaxed and have more fun yourself with a little help!

Make your guests feel welcome. You want them to sense an atmosphere of love at your party. Greet them at the door. Show them where they can put their coats and purses. Have something to nibble on as guests wait for everyone to gather. Introduce people who don't know each other. You might even want to have old-fashioned name tags made up in advance for everyone. Encourage the shy guests by introducing them to the more outgoing girls.

Don't allow anyone to feel left out. If someone has come to the party wearing the wrong clothing or shows up too early or too late, disregard it. They are probably embarrassed and the last thing they need is someone pointing out their mistake. A gracious hostess helps everyone have a good time and never makes a guest feel awkward or out of place. The simplest cure for a "minor mistake" is to tell your guest immediately how glad you are that they could be at your party!

A successful party will end with everyone feeling special because they have been welcomed and felt honored.

What to Wear to Your Party

A Victorian hostess was always dressed tastefully for the occasion. She would dress up, but she would not dress to outshine or compete with her guests. A beautiful attitude of hospitality was considered more important than wearing the prettiest outfit at the party!

One of the most enjoyable parts of giving a holiday party is the opportunity to dress up. You won't likely wear a corset, a bonnet, gloves, a bustle on your dress, or buttoned shoes like Elsie (though, for fun, you might want to!) but you can choose something that makes you feel special and pretty.

Here are some suggestions for what to wear for your old-fashioned Christmas party:

- *White lace blouses or collars*
- *Tartan plaid or satin sashes*
- *Taffeta or velvet dresses or skirts*
- *Hair ribbons*
- *Old-fashioned jewelry*
- *Full skirt with a swishy slip underneath*
- *Black patent leather shoes*
- *Christmas colors or colors to match the theme of the party*

Or you can make this a dress-up party with old costumes, shawls, vintage hats, Victorian jewelry, old party dresses, your mother's high heels, etc. It might be less "formal" but it might be more fun!

Decorating a Pretty Christmas Tree

There are many ways to decorate a Christmas tree. Like your party, your tree can have a theme. Some trees are decorated only in certain styles and colors, others are a jumble of many different things. Do you want a designer tree with coordinating colors and decorations tied to your party theme? Or would you like a nostalgic tree with things that are special to you or that represent special times in your past? Or you can have a tree with decorations that look like they could have been on Elsie's tree in the 1850s. Perhaps you want your tree to have nothing but homemade decorations. One sweet idea is a tree with lots of dolls of all sizes on and around it. Whether you choose a traditional red and green tartan theme, or a more feminine pink and white Victorian look, be creative and have fun decorating your tree!

Homemade Tree Ornaments

By the mid-to-late 1800s, the Christmas tree was a focal point of the Christmas celebration, but the people of Elsie's day did not have strands of electrical lights or the great variety of ready-made decorations to which we have become accustomed. They made their ornaments by hand using readily-available materials, such as paper, satin, lace, fabric scraps, ribbon, beads, cotton balls, and other odds and ends found around the house or grounds.

Trees in the Victorian era were lit with colored lamps and small candles wired to the branches. It was very common to decorate the tree with fresh and/or artificial flowers and fruit. Imagine seeing a tree with apples, oranges, pears, bananas, bunches of grapes, and other fruit hanging from its branches! Think how pretty a tree draped with roses, carnations, chrysanthemums, poinsettias, and other flowers would be. Strands of popcorn, nuts, berries, cookies, and candy were also used, as well as paper cornucopias filled with sweets and other goodies. Dolls and paper dolls were even nestled in the branches or hung on the tree, along with small or lightweight gifts tucked among the branches.

On the following pages are some simple, old-fashioned, homemade ornament ideas for you to consider. Remember, if you have chosen a color theme for your party, when you purchase supplies like ribbon and flowers, buy colors that will match your theme.

Doily Angels

Items Needed:

☐ 8" circle white cotton doilies (one per angel)

☐ 1 package of small rosettes (in pink or other color)

☐ Thin (3/16") ribbon (in pink or other color)

☐ Tootsie roll pops or other lollipops (one per angel)

☐ Glue stick or white glue

☐ Scissors

1. Cut ribbon into two sizes–one strip of approximately 12" in length and the other to match the diameter of your lollipop's head (each angel will require one ribbon of each size).

2. Find the back center of the doily. Put the head of the lollipop into the back center, drape the doily over it, and squeeze the doily around the head to the stem of the lollipop to create the "neck" of your angel. Then tie a strip of the 12" ribbon around the neck to secure the doily. (It is hard to tie the ribbon and hold down the doily by yourself, so you might need someone to help you with this part.) Tie it tightly, and then form a pretty bow.

3. Using your smaller strip of ribbon, wrap it around the top of the "head" of the angel to create a headband. Once you have figured out what position you like, then put glue on the back of the ribbon and glue it down in that position.

4. Glue a rosette onto the headband at the prettiest spot.

5. Set your angel on the tree!

Doily Snowflake

Items Needed:

☐ 4" circle white paper doilies

☐ Thin ribbon cut into strips of approximately 7" each

☐ Rosettes

☐ Glue stick or white glue

1. Make a loop with your ribbon and securely tape or glue the two ends next to each other on the back of a doily.

2. Glue a rosette onto the front of the doily just below the ribbon.

3. Hang your snowflake on the tree!

Paper Dolls and Paper Doll Chains

Items Needed:

☐ Construction paper or cardboard

☐ Scissors

☐ Optional: White glue or glue stick, crayons, markers or colored pencils, small bows, scraps of fabric, small buttons, bows, pieces of lace, beads, tiny silk flowers, scraps of floral wallpaper, glitter, thread, magazine photos, etc.

Draw your own picture of a doll onto construction paper or cardboard or cut out pictures of old-fashioned looking girls from magazines and then glue them onto construction paper or cardboard. Then cut out your doll and color and "decorate" her. Give her a Victorian-looking dress, hat, gloves, pantaloons, shoes, etc., by gluing on bows, buttons, lace, fabric, wallpaper scraps, etc. When you are finished, stand her on the branches of the tree, or poke a tiny hole at the top of her head and hang her using an ornament hook. Or use a hole punch to make a hole in the top of each paper doll, thread through a piece of thin ribbon, and tie the ends of the ribbon into a pretty bow, leaving a loop with which to hang your doll on the tree.

To make a paper doll chain, here are two options. First, make a number of individual paper dolls and use needle and thread to string them together like a chain. Then drape the chain on the tree. Or, take a very long piece of paper and fold it like an accordion. (To check yourself, the paper should fan out in even-sized sections.) Keeping the paper folded like that, draw or trace your doll design on the top flap of your accordion only. Make the arms of your doll reach all the way to the edge of the paper on both sides. Carefully cut it out, but be sure that you don't cut through the folded edge of the paper. Then open it up and you should have a garland of dolls — holding hands — to drape across your tree. Use crayons, markers, lace, fabric, glitter, and other items to decorate them in old-fashioned style.

Note: If you have real dolls that are lightweight enough, stand them on the branches of the tree!

Dated Ornament Balls

Items Needed:

- ☐ Clear glass ornament balls
- ☐ Ribbon - in a size to match the size of your ornament balls (if you use large balls as we did, then you should use 1-1/2" wide ribbon; if your balls are smaller, then use thinner ribbon)
- ☐ A gold metallic pen or acrylic paint and a brush
- ☐ Ornament hooks or twist ties   ☐ Scissors

1. On one side of your ornament ball, use your metallic pen or your paint and brush to write the date and, if desired, a brief message on the ornament ball, such as "Christmas 2000" or "Merry Christmas 2000" or "Elsie's Christmas Party 2000". Allow it to dry completely.

2. Once the first side is dry, then write whatever you want on the other side of the ornament– your name, your friend's name, or perhaps a Scripture verse. Allow it to dry completely.

3. Tie a pretty bow on the top of the ornament.

4. Hang the ornament on your tree using an ornament hook or twist tie.

Paper Star Ornaments

Items Needed:

- ☐ Brown or white paper bags   ☐ Scissors
- ☐ Glue stick or white glue   ☐ Twine
- ☐ A drawing or picture of a star

1. Create a stencil of your star by cutting it out from your drawing or picture.

2. Use your stencil to trace the shape on your paper bag and cut it out.

3. Cut a piece of twine about 12" long (one or two for each star).

4. Make a loop with your twine and glue the two ends of the twine down at the top back of your star. (Press the ends firmly and make sure they dry.)

5. Hang your star on the tree!

Snowmen and Snowball Ornaments

Items Needed:

☐ I package of cotton balls or cosmetic puffs

☐ Thin ribbon cut in 12" strips

☐ White glue

☐ Pen or pencil for poking a hole through the cotton

☐ Scissors

1.   Take one cotton ball. Using a pencil or pen, and with the help of an adult, carefully poke a hole all the way through the center of the cotton ball from one side to another (be careful not to poke your finger).

2.   Thread your strip of ribbon through the hole in the center of the cotton ball until you reach the middle of the ribbon strip.

3.   Tie the two ends of the ribbon together and make a bow, leaving a large loop below the bow. (This is the loop by which your snowman or snowball will hang from the tree.)

4.   Once you have completed the first 3 steps, you have a cotton ball with a ribbon through it. Let's call this a "head." Make several more of these heads and then put them aside.

5.   For a Snowman - Take five cotton balls and glue them in the shape of a flower, with one cotton ball in the center and the others glued around it like petals except leave a space for one more petal. Then glue on one of your "heads" in the space for the final petal. Stand your flower straight up and down with the head on top and two of the petals as feet. You will see that it looks like a snowman. Then hang it on your tree! (Optional: use beads, ribbon and other items to make a face, bowtie and other features for your snowman.)

6.   For a Snowball - Take four cotton balls and glue them together, with two on top and two on the bottom. Let the glue dry. Then glue one of the "heads" on the top of your group of balls at the center. Once the glue dries, hold your snowball in your hand and scrunch it together to shape it like a ball. Use another strip of ribbon and form a small bow. Glue the bow on the top of the snowball, and hang it on your tree!

7.   For a modern touch, you can buy a can of colored glitter spray and use it on your cotton ball ornaments.

More Decorating Tips

For a feminine touch, insert silk or fresh flowers in various places on the tree.

For a nostalgic touch, stand photographs or old Christmas cards on the branches of the tree.

For a pretty touch, besides using fabric for table linens or as part of homemade ornaments or gifts, consider using fabric for other things. In the Victorian time, and even today, beautiful fabrics in all different colors and patterns are available for use in decorating and entertaining. You can be as imaginative as the Victorians were by thinking of fun ways to utilize fabric. Even small scraps of fabric can be used to add a creative touch. A few yards of beautiful fabric cut into sections can be tucked or draped in between the branches of your tree and/or used as a tree skirt. All fabric stores sell remnants at bargain prices, and if you find a good deal, this can be a wonderful way to add an especially charming, designer look to your Christmas tree.

Taffy, Gumdrop, or Popcorn Strands

Items Needed:

☐ A large, sturdy needle

☐ Thread of any color

☐ A package of salt water taffy or gumdrops or a bowl of popcorn (for extra fun, try other items for your strands like dried fruit, berries, etc.)

☐ Scissors

1. Thread your needle with a very, very long piece of thread (make it twice as long as you want your final strand to be). Put the two ends of the thread together so that your thread is doubled and tie a double knot at the end.

2. One by one, begin threading your candy or popcorn onto the string. Take your time and don't be discouraged if some pieces break or fall apart as you go — just eat those and use new pieces!

3. When finished, hang your strand on the tree!

Fresh Fruit Ornaments

Items Needed:

☐ Small apples, oranges, lemons, limes, or other fruit

☐ Eye hooks (or other sturdy looped hooks from the hardware store)

☐ Ribbon or twine or twist ties

☐ Scissors

1. Take an individual piece of fruit. Carefully screw a hook into the top of the fruit or at the core.

2. For a fancy touch, tie a bow at the base of the hook.

3. Attach a piece of ribbon or twine or a twist tie to the hook and hang the fruit on a sturdy branch of the tree!

(Optional: insert cloves into the fruit to give it an old-fashioned look and a holiday aroma. You can also place cinnamon sticks tied in bundles with pretty ribbon in various places on the tree — they look pretty and smell great too!)

Paper Chains

Items Needed:

☐ Construction paper (red and green or, if desired, other colors) or Christmas wrapping paper

☐ Glue stick or white glue or tape

☐ Scissors

1. Cut the paper into strips of equal width and equal length (3/4″ wide by 6″ long).

2. Take one strip of paper and connect the two ends together with a small overlap using glue or tape.

3. Interlace a second strip into the first strip. Then connect the two ends of that second strip together with a small overlap using glue or tape. These two strips form the first two links in your chain.

4. Continue interlacing additional strips in the same way until your chain is the length you desire.

5. Then hang your chain on the tree!

Cookie Ornaments

Items Needed:

☐ Cookies (store-bought or homemade)

☐ Ribbon

☐ Scissors

1. If you are using store-bought cookies, then buy either ones with a hole in them (as we did) or (with adult supervision) carefully poke a hole in the cookies with a sturdy toothpick.

2. Cut a 12" strip of ribbon and thread it through the hole in the cookie.

3. Tie the two ends of the ribbon together leaving a large loop.

4. Hang your cookies on the tree! (Oops, you broke one. You know what to do!)

Gift Giving

When you are a guest at someone else's party, isn't it fun to receive a small gift that you can take home? It is that extra touch that reminds you that your presence was important to the hostess.

Here are some ideas for small gifts or "party favors" you can make for the guests at your Christmas party. It is a good idea to make your gifts well in advance, so that you are free to focus on other details as it gets close to the date of the party. Remember, it is more blessed to give than to receive, and even these small tokens of your love can serve as a reminder of the greatest gift of all–God's gift to mankind of the Savior, Jesus Christ.

Christmas Crackers

Items Needed:

☐ Empty toilet paper rolls or an empty roll of wrapping paper cut up into 4-1/2" mini-rolls

☐ Christmas wrapping paper

☐ Ribbon cut into approximately 12" long strips

☐ Scissors ☐ Tape or glue

☐ Small pieces of candy, gum balls, or other small goodies that will fit inside the roll

1. Cut a piece of wrapping paper that is wide enough to completely wrap around your roll and about 5" longer than your roll.

2. Center the roll on your piece of wrapping paper so that the amount sticking past the roll on each end is equal (extending approx. 2-1/2" from each end).

3. Secure the wrapping paper around the roll by taping or gluing it.

4. Tie a strip of ribbon tightly around the paper just beyond the end of the roll on one end only and then make a bow.

5. From the open end of the roll, fill the inside of the roll with candy or other goodies.

6. Tie a ribbon around the open end to secure it and make a bow.

7. Give them to your guests to open later.

Button Boxes

Items Needed:

☐ A large assortment of old buttons (you can purchase inexpensive bags full of assorted buttons from most craft stores)

☐ Small unpainted cardboard boxes (also available in craft stores)

☐ White glue or glue stick

☐ Pretty ribbon in various widths

☐ Scraps of lace or paper doilies

☐ Scissors

☐ Optional: small rosettes, beads, or other decorative sewing items

1. Choose one of the boxes and select pieces of lace or a doily that will cover the top of it. Cut or trim your lace or doily to fit. Once you have determined the best position for the lace or doily, glue it down and allow the glue to dry. If you don't have lace or doilies, you can skip this step and start with the next one.

2. Decorate the top of the box by gluing all kinds of buttons down in whatever creative pattern you want. If you are gluing them on top of a lace or doily background, you can use fewer buttons, but if you are gluing them onto a blank box top, you will need to have lots of buttons to cover the entire top. Either way, be sure to allow the glue to dry completely. If you have rosettes, beads, or other decorative sewing items, you can mix them in with your buttons.

Note: To glue down buttons, they need to have a flat back. Some buttons come flat, while others have a plastic loop on the back. If you want to use some that have the loop, you have two choices. You can have an adult cut the loops off the back of the buttons using wire cutters. Or using a pencil or pen, poke a very small hole in your cardboard box right in the spot where the button is to go. Then press the loop of the button into that hole until the main part of the button lies flush against the box. Once you are sure that it works, then remove the button, put glue on the back of it and press it on again.

3. Decorate the sides and bottom of your box by wrapping them with pretty ribbon (in one or more sizes). Once you have found the right position for your ribbon and trimmed it to fit, then glue it down and allow the glue to dry.

4. Finally, glue on more buttons to fill in any gaps or bare spots. Just like on the top of your box, you can mix in rosettes, beads, or other decorative sewing items with your buttons. Allow all the glue to dry completely.

5. Optional: fill the box with candy, potpourri, or other small goodies.

Verse Cards

1. Buy or make pretty note cards (one for each guest).

2. Pray and ask the Lord to help you choose a different verse of Scripture or promise from the Word of God for each person.

3. On the front of each person's card, write "A Special Message Just For _____" and fill in the name of the person.

4. On the inside of each card, in your prettiest handwriting, write out that person's verse or promise and the day, month and year. Sign the card and, if you like, you can also add a few words about why you feel that verse or promise is especially for her.

5. Either hide the cards under the dinner plates (for an after–dinner surprise) or hand them out before your guests leave at the end of the party. It will mean so much to your guests to know that you took time out from your busy preparations to reflect on them personally.

Candy Sachets

Items Needed:

- ☐ Lace or colored netting (known as tulle in the fabric stores)
- ☐ Old-fashioned hard candies or other kinds of candy that come in small pieces
- ☐ Thin ribbon
- ☐ Scissors

1. Cut the lace or netting into 12" squares.

2. Cut the ribbon into strips of approximately 12" in length.

3. Put a handful of candy into the center of the square of lace or netting. Pull up all four corners together.

4. Tie the sachet with ribbon to close it, but before it is tied too tightly, you (or preferably another person) will need to slip a second strip of ribbon underneath the first one at the back of the sachet and pull this second strip through until both ends are equal. This second strip is going to form the loop to hang your candy sachet on the tree. Once this is done, then tie your original strip of ribbon tightly and make a bow.

5. Tie the two ends of the second strip of ribbon together in a bow, leaving a large loop below it.

6. Make a candy sachet for each guest and hang them on the tree. At the end of the party, let each of your guests take one off the tree and keep it as a gift.

Dated Ornament Balls

Make a Dated Ornament Ball (see previous section) for each guest and write their name on the ball. Set each guest's ball on or by their dinner plate and let them keep it as a party favor. Or, hang the balls on the tree. At the end of the party, let each guest find and take theirs home as a memento!

Gift Wrapping

Once you've put all that work and thought into an appropriate gift for your guests, you may want to wrap them.

Not all gifts require wrapping, of course. But for those that do, find a box that is an appropriate size. Use tissue paper inside the box to keep the gift from being damaged. Wrap the outside of the box with store-bought or home-made wrapping paper. Then decorate the top of the box with some of the fancy ribbon, lace, greenery, flowers, bows, and/or other things you used for your party decorations. (Don't be afraid to cut those items into smaller pieces where necessary.) Use glue or tape to secure your decorations to the box.

Tip: Here's another decorating tip to add more Christmas color and cheer to your party. If you like gift-wrapping and you want to decorate under your Christmas tree or around the house, find some empty boxes of different shapes and sizes. Wrap them up as if they were real Christmas presents. Decorate them with flowers, fancy bows and other pretty things, and then set them under your tree or in places around the room. No one will know they are empty!

Decorating a Pretty Table

You can recreate the spirit of Victorian elegance with a beautifully set table. Linen, lace, flowers, ribbons, pretty china and sparkling glassware will bring a lovely Victorian flair to your party table. You will find that making your table beautiful is creatively satisfying and provides a welcoming atmosphere for guests. When it comes to setting your table, it might help inspire you if you think of yourself as not just setting it, but decorating it!

Table Linens

For an elegant look, select table linens that follow your color theme. For example, if you chose the red and green tartan theme for your party, then your tablecloth might be a solid red or solid green color or a tartan plaid. Or you might use a mixture by having a solid tablecloth with a tartan plaid table runner. If you chose the more feminine pink and white look, you could use a white lace tablecloth. A lace tablecloth looks even more elegant if you lay it over another cloth, which can be white or another color. If you prefer to use placemats, use handmade or store-bought ones that go with your color theme. For example, if your color theme is gold, then you might want gold placemats. In any case, adding cloth napkins instead of paper napkins will give the dressiest look.

Centerpieces

No formal Victorian table was complete without a centerpiece. Give careful thought to a colorful centerpiece that matches your theme. Red flowers such as poinsettias, roses, and carnations mixed with greens are beautiful and easy to work with. Many Victorians also decorated their tables with fruit bowls displaying seasonal bounty. Or you can even use something as simple as

a few beautifully wrapped Christmas packages for your centerpiece. Be creative! The centerpiece itself can be as simple or as elaborate as you like.

Sugared Fruit Centerpiece

Items Needed:

- [ ] fresh fruit—pineapple, apples, oranges, plums, pears, bananas, lemons, bunch of grapes, etc.

- [ ] bowl of raw egg whites (approx. 3)

- [ ] bowl of white sugar (approx. 2 cups)

- [ ] Whole English walnuts still in their shells (approx. 2 large handfuls)

- [ ] pastry brush

- [ ] large flat pan or cookie sheet

- [ ] a pedestal cake plate, a tall candlestick holder, a drinking glass, a regular plate, and/or other items that can be stacked together to form the layers of your centerpiece.

1. Determine what the arrangement of your centerpiece will look like, for example, how many levels you want it to have (three levels at most). Use the pedestal cake plate, the tall candlestick holder, the drinking glass, the regular plate, and/or any other items, to build the layers for your centerpiece. Be sure that it is stable.

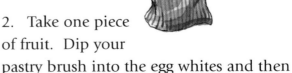

2. Take one piece of fruit. Dip your pastry brush into the egg whites and then

4. Coat and sugar all the pieces of fruit, one at a time, and place them on the pan/cookie sheet.

5. Sprinkle sugar over all of the fruit on the pan/cookie sheet.

6. Carefully take each piece of sugared fruit one at a time off the pan or cookie sheet and place it onto one of the levels of your centerpiece.

7. Use the walnuts to create a section of nuts or to fill in small spaces.

paint your piece of fruit. Coat it with egg whites all over.

3. Roll the coated piece of fruit in the sugar, coating it on every side, and then set it carefully on your pan or cookie sheet.

8. Optional: Finish it off with a fancy bow attached to your centerpiece by floral wire or twist ties.

Note:

Your sugared fruit centerpiece needs to be made the day of your party and preferably not more than a few hours ahead if you want it to look and stay fresh and so that the fruit can be eaten. If you can't or don't want to go through the messy, time consuming sugaring process, you can simplify things and and still have a beautiful centerpiece of fresh fruit. Simply skip the steps that have to do with coating and sugaring.

Other Table Decorations

Regardless of the centerpiece you use, you will also want to consider having other decorations for your table. Greenery will make your table look full and festive. Something that gives a beautiful holiday look is to put lots of greenery and garland down the whole center of the table. Then add flowers and/or fruit to this greenery and weave pretty ribbon through it.

And don't be afraid to separate or cut large pieces of greenery, garland, flowers, or ribbon into smaller sizes which can be used in multiple places. Also, be creative in your use of ribbon. You can, for example, combine two styles of ribbon to create a fancy look (as we have done by combining an off-white, lace-trimmed ribbon with pink ribbon).

Menu Cards and Place Cards

Dress your table up with place cards to assign seating around the table. You will need one place card for each person. If you want to make an extra effort, you can write the menu out by hand on individual menu cards. They will make lovely remembrances of your party. You can either make a few menu cards to be set about on the table, or you can make one for each guest. The following instructions are for making matching place cards and menu cards in a style that uses ribbons, bows and buttons. If you would prefer something simpler or you don't have much time, you can skip the steps that have to do with the ribbons, bows and buttons. In that case, you might want to use cards that already have a design on them, or draw your own elegant design, or decorate them with classy, Victorian-style stickers.

Items Needed:

- ☐ Blank note cards (that fold to form a tent where the front of the tent measures approx. 5-1/2" by 4-1/4")

- ☐ Felt tip, metallic or calligraphy pen in black, gold or another color

- ☐ Scissors

- ☐ Glue stick or white glue

- ☐ Red and green thin ribbon - 1/8" wide (or other colors to match your theme)

- ☐ Red and green tartan ribbon - 1/2" wide (or other colors to match your theme)

- ☐ Buttons in a color(s) that coordinates with your ribbon

Menu Cards

1. Determine how many menu cards you will need and make sure that you have enough blank cards to use (have a few extras on hand in case of mistakes). Fold the blank cards in half so they form tents.

2. Cut a strip of tartan ribbon to the exact height of the front of your card. Then glue the tartan ribbon to the card as a vertical stripe down the left edge of the card (either right at the edge or a little bit in from it).

3. Cut two strips of equal length (approx. 12″) of your red and green thin ribbons. Hold them together and then tie them in a bow. Glue the bow down onto your tartan ribbon about 1/4″ below the top of the card.

4. At the center just under the bow, glue on a button.

5. On the front of the card, in the area to the right of the tartan ribbon, write out the menu information for your party. (First practice on a piece of paper so that you know how to space out all of the words.) Write the menu items down in the order that you plan to serve them, with appetizers first and dessert last and everything else in between.

6. Set your finished menu cards on the table.

Place Cards

1. Determine how many place cards you will need (one per guest). Cut a blank card or heavy paper into a piece that is 2-3/4" by 4-1/4" and then fold it in half to form a small tent. (Be sure that the paper is heavy enough for the tent to stand on its own.)

2. Cut a strip of tartan ribbon to the exact width of the front of your card.

3. Glue the tartan ribbon to the card as a horizontal stripe along the bottom edge of the card.

4. At the far right or left corner of the tartan ribbon, glue on a pretty button.

5. On the front of the card, in the area above the tartan ribbon, write out the first name of your guest.

6. Make a place card for each guest.

7. Set your finished place cards on the table at the places where you want each guest to sit.

China and Dishes

China or pretty dishes will give your table the maximum elegance, but there are beautiful paper plates with coordinating napkins in a variety of patterns that can also give you a marvelous Victorian look. Be creative. Your china or dishes do not necessarily need to match. You can mix a variety of patterns – even going as far as to use a different pattern for each place setting – and still achieve a stylish look. For a pretty look that leaves more room for table decorations, you may want to place the salad plates on top of the dinner plates. If you use china, another simple thing that will add a lot of holiday elegance to the table is the use of "charger plates." Charger plates are extra large plates with very large rims so that dinner plates may sit on them. Charger plates are removed before the main course is served.

Silverware

The Victorian dinner table was filled with all sorts of silverware and utensils, each of which had a special use. Your table need not be so formal, but you can have a more Victorian look by adding a few pieces of silverware that you might not normally use. Consider adding a salad fork to the left of the dinner fork and a dessert spoon set horizontally above the dinner plate. These two simple additions can make your guests feel like they are being entertained at a royal table!

Tea or Coffee Cups

An easy idea that will give you an elegant, Victorian appearance is to use the tea/coffee cups as a part of your decoration. Of course, you can only do this if you will not be serving hot beverages. Fill the cups with water and then add in each cup a floating flower or a small floating candle called a "tea light". (Do not under *any* circumstances light candles without adult permission and supervision.)

Napkin Folding

These days there are many books that will show different creative napkin-folding ideas. Here is a very simple one. Open your napkin to a full square. Then fold it in half and make it into a triangle. Turn your triangle so that the base of the triangle is in front of you and the peak of the triangle is above it, pointing away from you. From the top layer only, take the corner and fold it halfway back so that it is pointing toward you. Keeping it in that position, turn the whole napkin over. Then take the right and left corners and fold them in.

Now turn the napkin back over and you will see that it has a fold that forms a pocket. If you are having rolls, for a fun touch, tuck one in each pocket!

Decorating a Pretty Room

The Victorian era was a time of decorating excess, meaning that Victorians loved to decorate lavishly and elaborately all over their homes. In addition to creating a beautiful Victorian-looking table, you might consider decorating a few other places in your dining room and home to coordinate with your table decorations. Use your imagination and be creative in spreading Christmas cheer!

Chair Decorations

Decorating the chairs at your table is easy and fun, and will add an unusually elegant touch to your party. Simply tie a large piece of wide, pretty ribbon on the back of each chair. You can tie it in a bow or leave it plain, and dress it up even more by using floral wire or twist ties to add flowers and/or greenery.

Punch Bowl Decorations

At a Victorian party, you would probably see a separate table with a punch bowl on it. If you have one at your party, remember to decorate this table too using your greenery, flowers and/or fruit.

Chandelier Decorations

Victorians loved beauty. And beauty does not need to stop at eye level. For a unique, Victorian touch that will really stand out, consider decorating the light fixture above your dining table with your greenery, flowers and/or fruit. (*Do not under any circumstances do this without adult permission and supervision.*) Top if off with fancy ribbon that goes with your color theme. Then enjoy watching your guests look up in surprise!

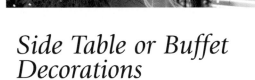

Side Table or Buffet Decorations

If there is a side table or buffet table in the room where you will be dining, remember to decorate it too. Doing so will help give your guests a sense of being surrounded by elegance and your party theme.

Front Door and Window Decorations

These days wreaths for your front door and windows can be readily purchased or easily made using Christmas ribbon, greenery, fruit, flowers, holly, and other decorative items. Buy one or be creative and make your own!

Mantle Decorations

At Christmas time in a Victorian home, the mantle would have been trimmed too. Like the Christmas tree, mantles were decorated with fruit such as pineapples, apples, oranges, plums, pears, bananas, lemons, and grapes, as well as pine, holly, poinsettias, other varieties of greenery and flowers, and brightly colored ribbon.

Menus and Recipes

One of the best things about a Victorian Christmas party was the food! Victorians loved to eat. Christmas dinner in a Victorian home was a long and delicious affair. Meals were often divided into courses or stages during which separate things were served. Unlike our meals, where we usually eat everything all at once, a formal Victorian dinner could have five to ten different courses! A Victorian dinner would have also featured a wonderful selection of desserts, such as the rich cream custard or the brightly colored fruit trifle that Elsie ate.

You might want to make the meal at your old-fashioned Christmas party a formal dinner. On the other hand, if you do not have the time or desire to go to all that trouble, an informal dinner or a lunch, brunch, afternoon tea or even dessert party would be just as appropriate and can be every bit as fun. Whatever you serve, in order to prevent last minute rushing, plan to do as much as possible ahead of time, including actually preparing some of the food in advance. But don't be afraid to have something cooking when the guests arrive—it will provide a delicious welcome.

We've included some examples of menus and recipes that you might like. We have selected menu items that will fit your holiday theme. You can make the food part of your party as simple or elaborate as you want — everything from a candlelight dinner in the grand Victorian style to a homemade pizza party. Formal Victorian entertaining would have included many fancy or gourmet foods that involved a great deal of preparation. If you are interested in those types of recipes, dozens of cookbooks include them.

Remember that this is your party — so make some of your own favorite dishes! If you have a family casserole recipe, a favorite Christmas cookie recipe, a special cake you love, or a delicious appetizer, by all means make it for this party. And be creative!

Menu Themes

The following are five different sample menus along with their corresponding recipes. Some of the recipes are easy and some are hard. You can use them, adapt them, mix and match them, or scrap them altogether and create your own menu plan!

- *Candlelight Dinner Celebration*
- *Sugar Plum Tea Party*
- *Cookie-Making Christmas Party*
- *Slumber Party Brunch*
- *Christmas Pizza Party*

Remember, when you are cooking or using candles in any manner, *always* have the supervision of an adult.

Candlelight Dinner Celebration

This is the grandest of all our menus and will no doubt require you to have the help of an adult. But that gives you a wonderful opportunity to do this project together with your parents and any other family members who want to be involved! This fancy dinner is the type of meal that would have been served at the Dinsmore home. It may require some extra work, but it will certainly make for a memorable Christmas Feast!

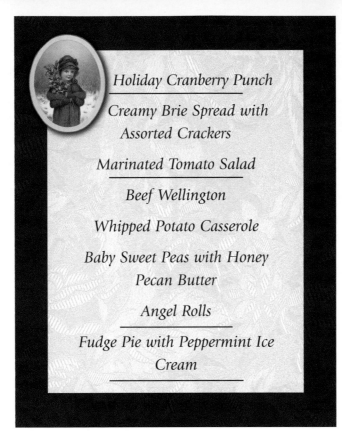

Holiday Cranberry Punch

Creamy Brie Spread with
Assorted Crackers

Marinated Tomato Salad

Beef Wellington

Whipped Potato Casserole

Baby Sweet Peas with Honey
Pecan Butter

Angel Rolls

Fudge Pie with Peppermint Ice
Cream

Holiday Cranberry Punch

1 package fresh cranberries

2 cups water

2 cups sugar

1 box (3 oz) orange gelatin

1 cup orange juice

2 liters ginger ale

Cook cranberries in 2 cups water until skin on cranberries pop. Drain cranberries and reserve juice. Using a wire sieve (or a very fine strainer), press the cranberries with a spoon through the wire mesh, reserving the cranberry pulp and discarding the skins. Bring cranberry pulp, 2 cups sugar, and reserved juice to a boil. Remove from heat. Dissolve orange gelatin in 1 cup boiling water. Add gelatin mixture to cranberry pulp and cool slightly. Add 1 cup orange juice and freeze the mixture. Remove from freezer 30 minutes before serving. Just prior to serving, add 2-liters of ginger ale. Gently mix. Punch is to have a slushy consistency.

Serves 8-12.

Creamy Brie Spread

4 oz. Brie cheese, softened

3 oz. package cream cheese, softened

1/2 tsp. seasoned salt

2 tbsp. sliced almonds

1 box assorted crackers

Line a 10 oz. custard cup or bowl with plastic wrap. Remove crust from Brie and discard the crust. Blend Brie, cream cheese and seasoned salt until smooth. Spoon into prepared cup; press firmly to pack. Fold ends of plastic wrap over to cover it. Refrigerate several hours or overnight to blend flavors. Unmold onto serving tray and remove plastic wrap. Press sliced almonds onto cheese.

Serve with assorted crackers.

Marinated Tomato Salad

4 cups romaine lettuce, torn

Marinade
1/4 cup oil
1 tbsp. sugar
3 tbsp. white wine vinegar
2 tbsp. chopped fresh parsley
2 tbsp. finely chopped green onions
1/8 tsp. garlic salt
1/4 tsp. basil leaves
Dash of oregano leaves
Dash of freshly ground black pepper
12 cherry tomatoes, quartered

Croutons
4 tbsp. butter
2 slices bread, cubed
1 clove garlic, minced
1/8 tsp. thyme leaves, crushed

Blend together marinade ingredients and add cherry tomatoes. Refrigerate at least 8 hours. Melt butter in a skillet. Add garlic, thyme, and bread cubes. Sauté until light brown and crisp. To serve, toss salad greens, marinade, and croutons together.   Serves 6.

Beef Wellington

3 lb. beef tenderloin roast	1/4 cup water
1/4 cup butter	2 tbsp. teriyaki sauce
1 lb. finely chopped fresh mushrooms	2 packages pie crust mix or 4 pie crust sticks, crumbled
1/2 cup finely chopped blanched almonds	1 cup dairy sour cream
1 clove garlic, crushed	1 egg, slightly beaten
	1 tbsp. water

Pre-heat oven to 425°F. Tie heavy string around roast in several places (this will keep it from curling up as it bakes and help it to bake evenly). Bake on a rack in a shallow baking pan. Bake 25 minutes for rare, 40 minutes for medium and medium-well, or 50 minutes for well-done. Cool on a wire rack for 30 minutes. Remove string and pat dry. In a large skillet, melt butter. Add mushrooms, almonds, garlic, water, and teriyaki sauce. Sauté over medium-high heat until liquid is absorbed. Set aside. Combine pie crust mix and sour cream and then mix with a fork until ball forms. On aluminum foil, roll out crust to measure a 20 x 12 in. rectangle. Reserve trimmed pieces of pastry. Place roast on edge of pastry; spread mushroom filling over pastry to within 1-inch of edges. Roll roast in pastry; seal the seam and ends by pinching together.

Place roast on a large greased cookie sheet with seam-side down. From the reserved pastry, cut out designs (such as holly leaves or lattice) and place them on the pastry-covered roast. Combine egg and water and brush over entire pastry. Bake at 400° F for 30 minutes or until golden brown. Allow to stand for 15 minutes before serving. For a pretty touch, garnish the platter with grapes, parsley, kale, or other decorative items.

Serves 8 to 10.

Whipped Potato Casserole

8 cups (2-1/2 lbs.) potatoes, peeled and cubed

1/2 cup mayonnaise

8 oz. cream cheese, softened

1 tsp. onion powder

3/4 tsp. salt

1/4 tsp. pepper

Dash of paprika

Cook potatoes until tender. Mash potatoes. Add mayonnaise, cream cheese, onion powder, salt and pepper. Whip potato mixture until fluffy. Place in a 1-1/2 quart casserole and garnish with paprika. Bake at 350° F for 45 minutes. May be made ahead and frozen. To serve, thaw casserole and bake at 350° F for 1 hour.

Serves 10-12.

Baby Sweet Peas with Honey Pecan Butter

1 (16 oz.) package frozen baby sweet peas

1 tbsp. butter

1 tbsp. honey

2 tbsp. coarsely chopped pecans

Prepare peas as directed on package. Drain well. Melt butter; add honey and pecans. Pour over peas and stir.

Serves 5.

Angel Rolls

4 cups self-rising flour

1/4 cup sugar

1 package dry yeast

2 cups warm water (120° to 130°F)

1 egg

3/4 cup vegetable oil

In a large bowl, combine flour, sugar, and yeast. Blend together warm water, egg, and oil. Add liquid ingredients to flour mixture and mix well. Spoon batter into greased mini-muffin cups.

Bake 15-20 minutes at 400° F. Batter will keep for several days in the refrigerator.

Makes 4 dozen mini rolls.

Fudge Pie

1 (9-inch) unbaked pie crust
2 squares unsweetened chocolate
1/4 cup butter
3/4 cup sugar
1/2 cup packed light brown sugar
1/2 cup milk
1/4 cup corn syrup
1 tsp. vanilla extract
1/4 tsp. salt
3 eggs
Peppermint or vanilla ice cream
Peppermint candies (crushed)

Preheat oven to 350° F. In a saucepan over low heat, melt chocolate and butter. Remove from heat. Add sugar, brown sugar, milk, corn syrup, vanilla, salt and eggs. Blend with a wire whisk until well mixed. Pour mixture into pie crust. Bake 45-55 minutes until filling is puffed. Cool (filling will shrink when cooled). Serve with ice cream. (Note: if you use vanilla ice cream, sprinkle crushed peppermint candies on top of it for a nice holiday touch.) Serves 8.

Sugar Plum Tea Party

Having a tea party was a very Victorian thing to do at any time of the year. So if you have a Victorian Christmas tea party, you will be very much in style — old-fashioned style, that is!

*Fresh Fruit with
Pineapple Dip*

*Miniature Orange Tea
Muffins*

Crepe Ham Pinwheels

Golden Cheese Triangles

Petal Tartlets

Poppy Seed Bread

*Tea Time Peanut Butter
Mice*

Assorted Teas

Fresh Fruit with Pineapple Dip

1 medium pineapple
1 egg, well-beaten
2 - 4 tbsp. sugar
1 tsp. all-purpose flour
1 cup whipping cream (whipped)
Other fresh fruit, cut in pieces

Cut a lengthwise slice off of the pineapple, removing about one-third of the pineapple. Cut and reserve the pineapple pulp from the slice and discard the rind. Scoop pulp from remaining portion of pineapple, leaving a shell that is 1/2 inch thick. Cube pineapple pulp into bite-size pieces. Crush 1 cup of pineapple pieces, reserving the juice. (Save the rest of the pineapple pieces for the fruit tray.) Mix the crushed pineapple, reserved juice, egg, sugar, and flour in a saucepan. Heat over low heat until thickened; cool. Fold in whipped cream. Spoon into pineapple shell. Serve with reserved pineapple chunks and other fresh fruit cut into pieces.

Miniature Orange Tea Muffins

1/2 cup orange juice
1 cup plus 2 tbsp. sugar
1 cup butter, softened
3/4 cup sugar
2 eggs
1 tsp. baking soda
3/4 cup buttermilk
3 cups all-purpose flour
1 tbsp. grated orange rind
1/4 cup orange juice
1 tsp. lemon extract
1 cup currants

In a saucepan, bring first 2 ingredients to a boil, stirring until sugar dissolves. Chill. Cream butter and gradually add 3/4 cup sugar. Beat until light and fluffy. Add eggs, one at a time. Beat well after each addition. Combine soda and buttermilk. Add to creamed mixture alternately with flour. Stir in orange rind, 1/4 cup orange juice, lemon extract, and currants. Fill greased miniature (1-3/4 inch) muffin pans 3/4 full. Bake at 400° F for 10-12 minutes. Remove from pans, dip top and sides of warm muffins in chilled sauce mixture. Allow to drain on wire racks. Makes 5 dozen.

Crepe Ham Pinwheels

1 (8 oz.) pkg. cream cheese, softened
3 tbsp. mayonnaise
1 tbsp. chopped chives
2 tsp. lemon juice
1/4 tsp. onion powder
1/4 tsp. dried whole dillweed
1/4 tsp. paprika
1/8 tsp. red pepper
12 (6-inch) packaged crepes
12 (4-inch square) slices of boiled ham

Using a mixer, blend first 8 ingredients. Spread a heaping tablespoon of filling evenly over each crepe. Place a ham slice over filling and roll-up crepe jelly-roll fashion.

Wrap and chill each crepe for at least 1 hour. To serve, slice each roll into 1/2 inch pieces.

Makes 7 dozen.

Golden Cheese Triangles

2 cups (8 oz.) shredded cheddar cheese

1 package (3 oz.) cream cheese, softened

1/4 cup mayonnaise

1/2 tsp. Worcestershire sauce

1/8 tsp. onion salt

1/8 tsp. garlic salt

1/8 tsp. celery salt

Thin-sliced bread with crusts removed

Mix first seven ingredients and chill.

(Will make 1-1/2 cups of filling.)

To assemble sandwiches, spread filling between two slices of thin-sliced bread (crusts removed).

Cut sandwich into four triangles to serve.

Makes 24 triangle-shaped sandwiches.

Petal Tartlets

1/4 cup shortening

1/4 cup butter, softened

1/2 cup sugar

1 egg

3/4 tsp. vanilla

1-1/2 cups all-purpose flour

1/2 tsp. salt

1/4 tsp. baking soda

Strawberry, cherry or apricot preserves

Mix shortening, butter, sugar, egg, and vanilla. Sift flour, salt and baking soda together and add to shortening mixture. Mix thoroughly. Refrigerate dough several hours or overnight. Preheat oven to 400°F. On a floured surface, roll dough to 1/8 inch thickness. Cut dough with a 3-inch round scalloped cutter. Ease rounds into mini-muffin cups and fill each with 1-1/2 tsp. of preserves. Bake 8-10 minutes. Cool slightly before removing from muffin pan.

Makes 36 tartlets.

Poppy Seed Bread

3 cups all-purpose flour
1-1/2 tsp. baking powder
1-1/2 cup milk
2-1/4 cup sugar
1-1/2 tsp. vanilla extract
1-1/2 tsp. almond extract
1-1/2 tsp. salt
3 eggs
1-1/3 cup oil
1-1/2 tbsp. poppy seeds

Combine ingredients in a bowl and mix for one minute. Pour batter into two greased bread pans and bake at 350° F for 45 minutes to 1 hour or until it tests done. Allow to cool in pans for 15 minutes. Turn bread out onto a rack and top with glaze.

Glaze

1/4 cup orange juice
3/4 cup powdered sugar
1/2 tsp. almond extract
1/2 tsp. vanilla extract

Beat ingredients together until smooth.

Tea Time Peanut Butter Mice

1/2 cup butter
1/2 cup peanut butter
1/2 cup sugar
1/2 cup brown sugar, packed
1 egg, well-beaten
1-3/4 cup all-purpose flour
3/4 tsp. baking soda
1/4 tsp. salt
1/2 tsp. baking powder
Peanut halves, red hot candies, and licorice shoelaces

Cream together butter and peanut butter. Gradually add sugars, beating until light and fluffy. Add egg and mix. Sift together flour, baking soda, salt, and baking powder. Add to sugar mixture. Blend well. Dough should be very stiff (if not, chill). With fingers, roll pieces of dough into walnut-sized balls. Pinch one end of ball to form a mouse nose. Place on a greased cookie sheet. Add red hot candy eyes and peanut half ears. Bake 5-8 minutes at 375° F or until lightly browned. Let cool slightly on cookie sheet until they may be easily removed. While cookie is still warm, add a licorice shoelace tail. Makes 4 dozen.

Share the Joy Cookie Baskets

It's fun to prepare baskets of homemade cookies for family and friends and for gifts to the poor or less fortunate in your community. Here are some tasty recipes you might wish to include, but for this type of "menu," you certainly will want to add your own favorite recipes too!

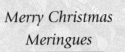

*Merry Christmas
Meringues*
_____

Brown Sugar Spritz
_____

Holly Leaf Cookies
_____

*No-Bake Ugly
Ducklings*
_____

Chocolate Snowballs
_____

Merry Christmas Meringues

2 egg whites, room temperature

Dash of salt

3/4 cup sugar

1 tsp. vanilla extract

1 (6 oz.) package chocolate chips

1 cup pecans, chopped

Preheat oven to 350° F. Beat egg whites until foamy; add salt. Gradually add sugar, one tablespoon at a time. Beat until stiff peaks form. Fold in vanilla, chocolate chips, and pecans. Drop by teaspoon onto foil-lined cookie sheet. Place cookies in the oven and immediately turn off heat. Allow to remain in the oven for eight hours. Do not open the door during this time.
Makes 4 dozen.

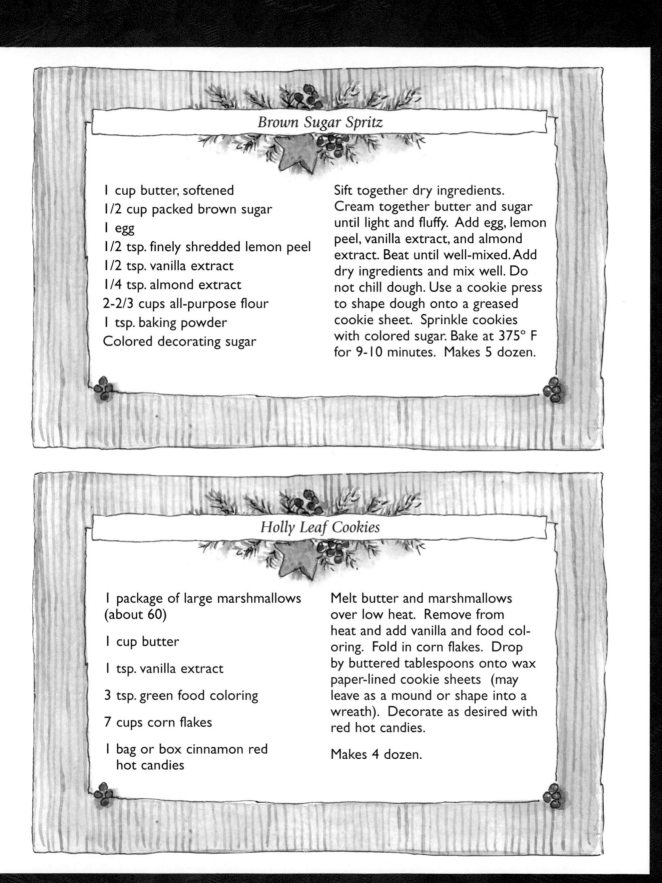

Brown Sugar Spritz

1 cup butter, softened
1/2 cup packed brown sugar
1 egg
1/2 tsp. finely shredded lemon peel
1/2 tsp. vanilla extract
1/4 tsp. almond extract
2-2/3 cups all-purpose flour
1 tsp. baking powder
Colored decorating sugar

Sift together dry ingredients. Cream together butter and sugar until light and fluffy. Add egg, lemon peel, vanilla extract, and almond extract. Beat until well-mixed. Add dry ingredients and mix well. Do not chill dough. Use a cookie press to shape dough onto a greased cookie sheet. Sprinkle cookies with colored sugar. Bake at 375° F for 9-10 minutes. Makes 5 dozen.

Holly Leaf Cookies

1 package of large marshmallows (about 60)

1 cup butter

1 tsp. vanilla extract

3 tsp. green food coloring

7 cups corn flakes

1 bag or box cinnamon red hot candies

Melt butter and marshmallows over low heat. Remove from heat and add vanilla and food coloring. Fold in corn flakes. Drop by buttered tablespoons onto wax paper-lined cookie sheets (may leave as a mound or shape into a wreath). Decorate as desired with red hot candies.

Makes 4 dozen.

No-Bake Ugly Ducklings

1 large bag chow mein fried noodles

1-1/2 cups peanuts or cashews

1 (12 oz.) package semi-sweet chocolate chips

1 (12 oz.) package butterscotch chips

Melt the chocolate chips and butterscotch chips together over low heat. When melted, remove from heat and slowly fold in the nuts. Then gently fold in the chow mein noodles. Drop by spoonfuls onto cookie sheet covered with wax paper. Refrigerate until the chocolate is completely hardened. Then peel them off the wax paper and enjoy.

Makes 3 dozen.

Chocolate Snowballs

3/4 cup firmly packed brown sugar
3/4 cup butter, softened
3 (1 oz.) squares of unsweetened baking chocolate, melted and cooled
1 tsp. vanilla extract
2 cups all-purpose flour
1/2 tsp. salt
1 cup chopped nuts (pecans, almonds, or walnuts)
2/3 cup sifted powdered sugar

Preheat oven to 350° F. Beat together brown sugar and butter until light and fluffy. Add melted chocolate and vanilla and beat until well mixed. Add remaining ingredients, except powdered sugar. Continue beating until well mixed. Shape rounded teaspoonfuls of dough into 1-inch balls and place 1/2-inch apart on ungreased cookie sheets. Bake 8-10 minutes, or until set. Cool five minutes on cookie sheets. Carefully remove from cookie sheets and cool five more minutes. Roll in powdered sugar while still warm and again when cooled.
Makes 5 dozen.

$\mathcal{S}$weet Dreams Slumber Party Brunch

After a night of pillow fights and little slumber, treat your friends to a good morning brunch. There is nothing like waking up to a hot meal, and with the addition of a few Christmas decorations to your table, you can all start the day in a festive mood!

Tutti Fruitti Fruit Cups

Overnight French Toast

Crisp Bacon Slices

Rise and Shine Surprise Muffins

Fruit Juices

Hot Chocolate

Milk

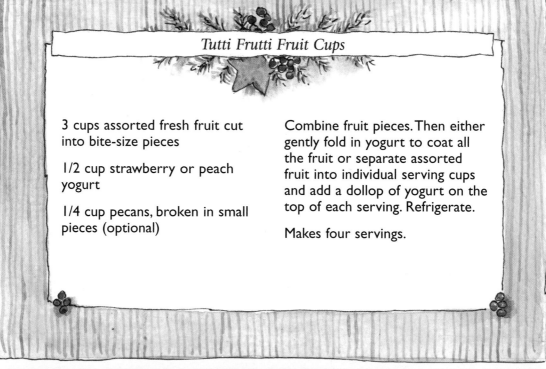

Tutti Frutti Fruit Cups

3 cups assorted fresh fruit cut into bite-size pieces

1/2 cup strawberry or peach yogurt

1/4 cup pecans, broken in small pieces (optional)

Combine fruit pieces. Then either gently fold in yogurt to coat all the fruit or separate assorted fruit into individual serving cups and add a dollop of yogurt on the top of each serving. Refrigerate.

Makes four servings.

Overnight French Toast with Crisp Bacon Slices

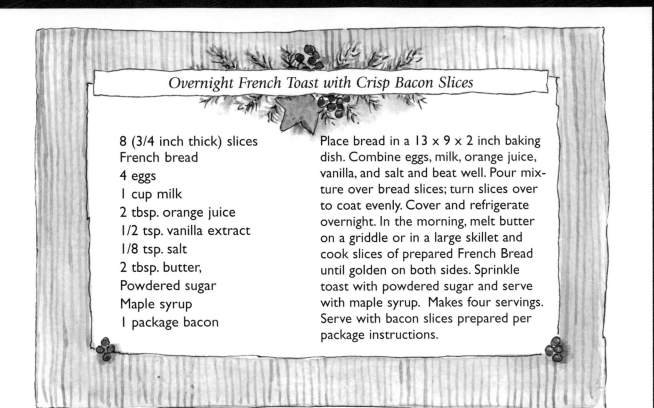

8 (3/4 inch thick) slices
French bread
4 eggs
1 cup milk
2 tbsp. orange juice
1/2 tsp. vanilla extract
1/8 tsp. salt
2 tbsp. butter,
Powdered sugar
Maple syrup
1 package bacon

Place bread in a 13 x 9 x 2 inch baking dish. Combine eggs, milk, orange juice, vanilla, and salt and beat well. Pour mixture over bread slices; turn slices over to coat evenly. Cover and refrigerate overnight. In the morning, melt butter on a griddle or in a large skillet and cook slices of prepared French Bread until golden on both sides. Sprinkle toast with powdered sugar and serve with maple syrup. Makes four servings. Serve with bacon slices prepared per package instructions.

Rise and Shine Surprise Muffins

1-3/4 cup all-purpose flour
1/4 cup sugar
2-1/2 tsp. baking powder
3/4 tsp. salt
1 well-beaten egg
3/4 cup milk
1/3 cup salad oil
1/4 cup jelly (your favorite flavor)

Sift dry ingredients into a bowl; make a well in the center. Combine egg, milk, and oil; mix well. Add liquid ingredients to dry ingredients. Stir just until dry ingredients are moistened. Fill paper-lined muffin cups 2/3 full. Top batter in each cup with 1 tsp. jelly. Bake at 400° F for 25 minutes, or until done.

Makes 12.

$\mathcal{S}$howtime Pizza Party

How about inviting your friends over to watch a
favorite Christmas video? Add to the fun by serving
Christmas tree-shaped pizzas that you and your
friends decorate with favorite pizza toppings.

Christmas Tree Pizzas

Crunchy Vegetable Bites
with Festive Vegetable Dip

Peppy Popcorn Snack

Yummy Chocolate
Brownie Sundaes

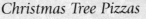

Christmas Tree Pizzas

1 can (16 oz.) tomato sauce
1 cup coarsely chopped tomato
1/2 tsp. dried oregano leaves
1/2 tsp. dried basil leaves
2 pkgs. (13-3/4 oz. each) hot roll mix
Assorted pizza toppings: shredded mozzarella and cheddar cheese, chopped red and green peppers, chopped onions, sliced pepperoni, sliced mushrooms, pineapple pieces, sliced olives, ham, etc.

Cover eight 7-inch paper plates completely with aluminum foil; grease lightly. Make hot roll mix according to package directions, but do not let dough rise. Divide dough into eight equal pieces. Spoon sauce and desired toppings into bowls. Allow each guest to shape pizza dough into a tree shape. Spoon approximately 3 tbsp. sauce on each pizza and decorate as desired. Place pizzas on a cookie sheet and bake at 375°F until crusts are golden brown, about 20 minutes. Makes 8 servings.

Crunchy Vegetable Bites with Festive Vegetable Dip

1 cup cottage cheese

1 cup sour cream

1 envelope dry Italian salad dressing mix

assorted fresh vegetables

Mix the first three ingredients together and serve with assorted fresh vegetables, cut into bite-size pieces.

Peppy Popcorn Snack

8 cups of popped popcorn
2-1/2 cups of miniature pretzels
2-1/2 cups corn crunch twist snacks
1/3 cup butter, melted
1 tsp. lemon pepper
1/2 tsp. oregano leaves
1/4 tsp. chili powder
1/4 tsp. garlic powder
1/4 tsp. onion powder

Heat oven to 325°F. Combine popcorn, pretzels, and corn twists. Melt butter; stir in seasonings and pour over popcorn mixture. Stir gently to coat. Spread mixture on an ungreased 15" x 10" jelly roll pan. Bake for 10 to 15 minutes, stirring once during baking.

Makes 11 cups.

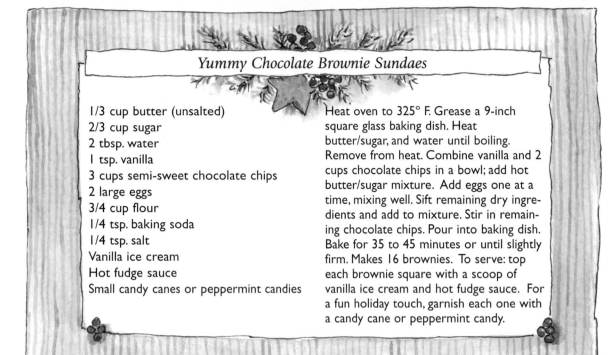

Yummy Chocolate Brownie Sundaes

1/3 cup butter (unsalted)
2/3 cup sugar
2 tbsp. water
1 tsp. vanilla
3 cups semi-sweet chocolate chips
2 large eggs
3/4 cup flour
1/4 tsp. baking soda
1/4 tsp. salt
Vanilla ice cream
Hot fudge sauce
Small candy canes or peppermint candies

Heat oven to 325° F. Grease a 9-inch square glass baking dish. Heat butter/sugar, and water until boiling. Remove from heat. Combine vanilla and 2 cups chocolate chips in a bowl; add hot butter/sugar mixture. Add eggs one at a time, mixing well. Sift remaining dry ingredients and add to mixture. Stir in remaining chocolate chips. Pour into baking dish. Bake for 35 to 45 minutes or until slightly firm. Makes 16 brownies. To serve: top each brownie square with a scoop of vanilla ice cream and hot fudge sauce. For a fun holiday touch, garnish each one with a candy cane or peppermint candy.

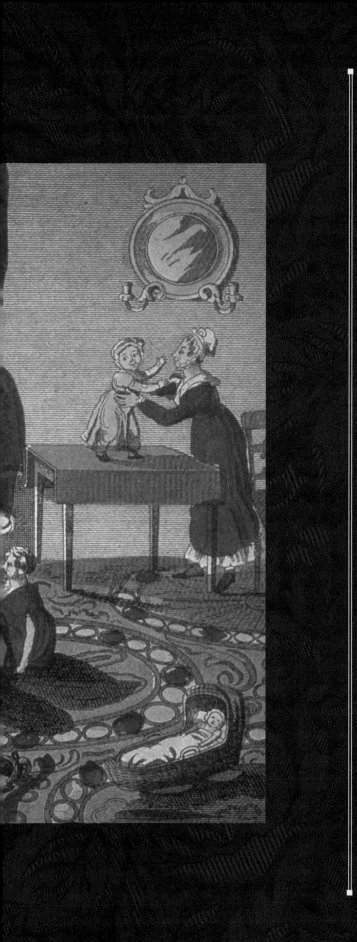

Old-Fashioned Entertainment

No Victorian party would be complete without entertainment. The purpose of the festivities was to meet with friends and families for fun and fellowship. Renewing acquaintances, lively conversation, a variety of music, fun parlor games and memorable readings were enjoyed by everyone as entertainment in those days. But that kind of memory-making event doesn't just happen!

Remember the hostess is responsible for making sure everyone feels comfortable and that no one is excluded, especially when it comes to the evening's entertainment. Thoughtful pre-party planning is very important — but don't be so "organized" that you leave no room for spontaneity! Have an attitude of love and think of the comfort and enjoyment of each of your guests. The party atmosphere always reflects the attitude of its hostess. If you are tense and nervous about keeping to a strict schedule of activities, it might not be as fun for anyone. If you are warm, loving and enthusiastic, your guests will respond with laughter and delight. If you plan well and keep an open mind, you just might have to turn out the lights to signal to your guests when the party is over — otherwise they might stay all night!

"Working" Fun

You might want the entertainment portion of your party to be centered around a craft-making or "working" activity time. Because of the season, it would be thoughtful to create some small, simple gifts for people who might not otherwise have Christmas joy. Think of retirement centers, homeless shelters, and other ministries. Your local church can provide you with suggestions for the greatest needs in your area. Use your imagination! Some ideas include:

- *baking Christmas cookies*

- *decorating a small Christmas tree*

- *making homemade Christmas ornaments*

- *making and/or wrapping Christmas gifts*

- *Christmas caroling*

- *making Christmas cards for others to send*

- *making hot cocoa mix or spiced tea mix*

- *making small gift baskets*

Determine in advance of the party what your "working" activity will be and be sure to have on hand all of the supplies

you may need. You will want your guests to know what to expect. For instance, if you're baking or doing some other "messy" craft, you might provide aprons for everyone. (Would you want to spoil a pretty party outfit?) Always think of your guests first, and the fun will follow!

Parlor Games

You may want the entertainment at your party to be the kind of old-fashioned games that Elsie might have played with her family and friends. In Elsie's time, these were known as "parlor games" because in the large, wealthy Victorian homes of Elsie's day, the "parlor" was the room where families would gather to entertain their guests.

Victorian "parlor games" were popular with all ages. They may seem silly or simple to us, but that was exactly why the Victorians enjoyed these types of games — they were easy enough for both the young and old to play and they were guaranteed fun for all. Besides, they were not distracted by television, computers, movies and the countless other modern-day entertainment options available to us today. Part of the fun of parlor games for us is that they are so old-fashioned they seem brand new!

The following are some parlor games that you might enjoy. You can choose a few of these games for your party, or you can be creative and make up your own! Many of these games have no "winner." The object is just to have fun!

The Concept Of Forfeits:

Victorians loved silliness in their games. And one way they found it was in making players who were "out" (or who lost) perform a "forfeit." A forfeit was a silly or embarrassing task that the person had to do as a penalty. The hostess can make up a list of forfeits in advance and write them on slips of paper placed into a bowl. Then, when needed, a player can draw a slip to determine their forfeit. Some examples might be:

- *dance around like a ballerina from the Nutcracker Suite*
- *whistle a Christmas carol*
- *sing and act out the song "Jingle Bells" (or for more fun change it to "Bingle Jells")*
- *make up 12 new gifts for the song "The 12 days of Christmas"*
- *recite a tongue twister 10 times very fast (such as "she sells seashells by the seashore")*
- *hop up and down and wave your arms while standing on one leg*
- *flap your arms and cluck like a chicken*
- *say your name spelled backwards*

or any other fun or silly act you can think of!

Hunt the Slipper

All of the players except for one sit in a circle (they are the "cobblers"). The person who is "It" (who is the "customer") stands in the center holding a "slipper" (a shoe of any kind). "It" then hands the shoe to one of the players and recites this rhyme: "Cobbler, cobbler, mend my shoe, Get it done by half past two." The customer then closes her eyes and counts to ten. While she is counting, the slipper is passed around the other players' backs. "It" is then told to open her eyes. She says to the player that she handed the slipper to, "May I have my slipper, please?" The player replies, "You must find it." The customer then has to guess who has the slipper and catch them with it at a given moment. (During this time, the players can still be secretly passing the slipper between them. The faster the slipper is passed, the harder it is for the customer to find. If they want to be really bold, they can toss it to each other when the customer's back is turned! When the cus-

tomer names a particular person, that person must immediately lift her hands. If the customer has guessed correctly, the person caught with the slipper then becomes "It." If not, "It" tries again.

Squeak, Piggy, Squeak

All the players except for the hostess sit in chairs arranged in a circle. The hostess, who will be "It," stands in the middle of the circle. She is given a pillow or cushion to hold with both hands and is then blindfolded and spun around a few times. The object of the game is for her to guess the identity of one of the other players by listening to the player squeal like a pig.

Holding the pillow or cushion in front of her, she must find her way to someone's lap, put the pillow on the lap and sit on it without touching the person. She then says, "Squeak Piggy, Squeak." The chosen person, disguising her voice, has to squeak like a pig. If "It" can't identify her after a few squeaks, "It" must move on to someone else's lap and try to guess their identity. When "It" correctly identifies a person, that person becomes "It."

Duck, Duck, Goose

The players sit facing each other in a circle on chairs (leave enough space between the chairs for a person to pass through). The hostess is "It" and walks around the outside of the circle, lightly tapping each player's head one by one and saying "duck, duck, duck." When she wants to, she taps someone's head and says "goose" and that person must then chase her all the way around the circle to try to tap her before she gets back to the goose's empty chair. If she sits in the empty chair before getting tapped, then she is safe and the goose becomes "It", and the game continues. If the goose does tap her before she gets to the chair, she has to stand in the middle of the circle and perform a "forfeit" before becoming "It" again and starting over trying to unseat a goose.

Things That Have a Story

Before the party, the hostess selects a number of small items from around 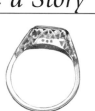 the house (at least as many items as there will be people at the party) and places them on a table or tray. Some examples are a pen or pencil, paper clip, hat, hair accessory, piece of jewelry, a kitchen utensil, a picture, a candle, a bowl of potpourri, etc. Whoever is chosen to be first begins by picking an item and making up a short statement about why that item was important in history. For example, she might say, "This paper clip might look like an ordinary paper clip, but it's actually the paper clip that held the pages of the Declaration of Independence together!" Then one by one, each person has to add a statement to the story using a new item, but also restating the previous facts in reverse order. So the second person might say, "This is the candle that lit the room when Thomas Jefferson signed the Declaration of Independence whose pages were held together by that paper clip." The third person could then say, "This is the potpourri that scented the room that was lit by the candle that was in the room when Thomas Jefferson signed the Declaration of Independence whose pages were held together by that paper clip." And on it goes. (You can tell that being the last person in this game is really difficult — but fun!)

Make a Will

When a person dies, they generally leave behind a will, which is a legal paper that tells people what to do with their possessions. For this game, the hostess will begin by telling each person in the room one thing that she will leave to them in her imaginary will. For example, she might leave one person her smile, another her eyelashes, someone else her favorite shoes, another her hairbrush, someone else her common sense, etc. She then picks a person to go next. That person tells what they are leaving to who, and then they pick the person to go next. And on it goes. You'd be surprised how sweet and fun this game can be!

String-a-Long

For this game, you will need a roll of string or a ball of colored yarn or a spool of colored ribbon. Before the party, the hostess should unroll it and cut it into 50 to 100 pieces of different lengths. She should then

hide each piece someplace in the room or rooms that will be "the territory" for the game. When the game starts, divide the players into teams (a minimum of two teams). Explain where the territory begins and ends and tell the players that you have hidden pieces of string or yarn or ribbon in different lengths all throughout the territory. Each team has to find and tie together as many pieces as possible. The hostess will say when the teams should start and stop searching (she can set a timer and have the players stop searching when the timer goes off or just say "Stop!" when she feels all the pieces have probably been found). The team with the longest tied-together line at the end of the game is the winner. (Hint: the smaller the knots the better chance you have of winning!)

Hide and Find

The hostess selects a small object that will be hidden in this game, such as a piece of candy or a button, and shows it to everyone. Then everyone leaves the room and the hostess "hides" the object somewhere in the room in plain view. The guests are called to return to the room. The hostess says "go" and everyone beings hunting. Whoever finds the object gets to be the one to hide it next.

❦

Ducks That Fly

The group selects a leader. The players stand in a circle with the leader in the middle. When the leader says, "ducks fly" and flaps her arms, all the players must flap their arms. If she says "dogs bark," and barks like a dog, all the players must do the same. If she says, "birds chirp" or "cows moo" or "cats meow," the players must imitate her sound or motions. But whenever she wants, she can make a false statement, such as "cats bark" or "cows fly." If any player imitates the false sound or motion, she is "out" and has to perform a "forfeit."

The Cat's Concert

Divide people into groups of three or four each. One at a time, each group will perform for the other groups (who will act as their audience). But in this concert, the group members each sing a different song

all at the same time. The "winner" is the funniest performance!

Change Seats

All of the players except for one sit in chairs in a circle. The object of the game is for "It" to get a seat in the circle. To begin the game, "It" stands in the center and calls out, "Change seats" as many times as she likes. The players, however, stay in their seats until she adds the phrase "The King's Come!" When the other players hear these words, they must all change seats except they cannot take the seat to the right or left of them. "It" tries to get a seat for herself. If she succeeds, the person left standing becomes "It" for the next round.

Charades

The group is divided up into teams. The object of the game is to get the other members of your team to correctly guess the most words or phrases from seeing them acted out silently. Depending on the age and skill of your guests, you can determine in advance how difficult you want the words or phrases to be. They can be short words or more complicated phrases or titles. You can write out the words on slips of paper in advance and put them in a bowl for the teams to draw from. The words can be names of movies, books, things, actions, animals, etc. Choose words that everyone will know. If you choose words that are from various categories, then you should allow the team acting out the word to tell or indicate the category. To start the game, one player draws a slip from the bowl and tries to communicate what is on it to his teammates by acting it out in total silence. Hand signs and acting gestures can be used. If the team correctly guesses the word in the designated amount of time, then they get a point for their team. The teams alternate turns.

NOTE: If you decide to have winners and prizes for your games, don't let anyone go home without having received something — even if that something is a personal hug and special thank you from the hostess. Make them feel like a winner even if it wasn't a game that they won!

Christmas Carols

Music was also a very important part of Victorian entertainment, especially at Christmas time. We can imagine Elsie's friends and loved ones gathered around the piano in the parlor room singing Christmas carols, with a fire brightly burning in the fireplace, cups full of hot spiced cider, and voices blended together in sweet harmony and joyful praise.

You might want to sing some Christmas carols at your Christmas party. Besides being fun, this will also help create a worshipful atmosphere and will set the stage for a time of Christmas readings. If you do decide to have carols at your party, you should prepare a list of the carols you would like to sing in advance. Even though during the party you may decide to add others, this will help you to be prepared. If you have access to Christmas carol lyric sheets, you should have several copies on hand for you and your guests to share.

Christmas Readings

Victorian parlor entertainment also included readings and story-telling. People would read aloud poetry, selections from the Bible or other favorite books, or recite or perform their own made-up stories.

Memorizing poetry and other literary material and reciting it before family and friends was part of every child's education, but parlor gatherings and parties offered an opportunity to add extra dramatic effect to such presentations!

For your old-fashioned Christmas party, you might select a few readings with Christmas themes. Perhaps a piece of Christmas poetry or a Christmas short story. You might even want to ask your guests ahead of time to bring along their favorite Christmas readings. Christmas readings can be long or short, serious or light-hearted, or a mixture of each.

There are many wonderful Christmas stories from the past, such as Charles Dickens' classic tale, *A Christmas Carol,* written in 1843. But there are also many Christmas stories written in our day that when read aloud can sound very "old-fashioned." You have many more literary works to choose from than Elsie did!

Here are just a few examples:

The Legend of the Candy Cane by Lori Walburg (Zondervan Publishing House, 1997); the chapter called "An Intimate Moment with Mary and Joseph" from the book, *Intimate Moments with the Savior* by Ken Gire (Zondervan Publishing House, 1989); the book, *This is the Star* by Joyce Dunbar and Gary Blythe (Scholastic Inc., 1996); *The Tale of Three Trees* by Angela Elwell Hunt (Chariot Victor, 1989); *The Littlest Angel* written by Charles Tazewell in 1957; and *The Secret of the Gifts* by Paul Flucke (InterVarsity Press, 1982). You may well have other favorites or would like to write your own story about the season! Plus, you might want to research the legends of the holly and the ivy, the dogwood tree, the poinsettia, the sand dollar, and other symbols of Christmas, and share them at your party. Check your church or public library or the Internet.

There are also many poems about Christmas that you can plan to have recited at your party. For example, Christina Rosetti wrote the following poem in the fifteenth century. It is the kind of poem you might have heard at Elsie's Christmas party and it would be perfect for a brief recitation at your party. It is about the simplest, but most important, gift we can give at this blessed season.

What Can I Give Him?

What can I give Him, poor as I am?
If I were a shepherd, I would bring a lamb
If I were a rich man, I would do my part
Yet, what can I give Him?
Give Him my heart.

As another example of poetry that you could read, here is a poem written by Phillips Brooks (1835-1893) during the American Civil War. Notice the references to the varied landscapes of America — North and South — in the first stanza. The second stanza is a clear reference to the battles that were raging — even at Christmas. And yet, there is always hope with Jesus!

Christmas Everywhere

Everywhere, everywhere, Christmas
tonight!
Christmas in lands of the fir-tree
and pine,
Christmas in lands of the palm-tree
and vine,
Christmas where snow peaks stand
solemn and white,
Christmas where cornfields stand
sunny and bright.

Christmas where children are hopeful
and gay,
Christmas where old folks are patient
and gray,
Christmas where peace, like a dove in
his flight,
Broods o'er brave men in the thick of
the fight.

Everywhere, everywhere, Christmas
tonight!

For the Christ-child who comes is the
Master of all,
No palace too great, no cottage too
small.

Everywhere, everywhere, Christmas
tonight!

A Partridge in a Pear Tree

When you think of the familiar seasonal favorite, "The Twelve Days of Christmas," you may have wondered what a partridge in a pear tree has to do with the birth of our Lord? This fun song may be somewhat difficult to memorize, but it has a fascinating history that you might want to share with the guests at your party.

The Story Behind the Song

The time between Christmas Day and Epiphany, a Catholic festival observed on January 6th, is twelve days. "Epiphany" literally means revelation, manifestation, or a sudden knowledge. It celebrates the journey of the three wise men who followed the star to Bethlehem to meet Jesus, the promised Savior of mankind.

In England, from the mid-1500s to 1829, it was against the law for Catholics to practice their faith in public or in private. Those that were caught could be brutally treated, imprisoned or executed. But because many Catholic people held such strong beliefs — regardless of the strict laws of their time — they still wanted to teach the basics of their faith to their children. One of the clever ways they did it was through the song "The Twelve Days of Christmas." It must have seemed like nothing more than a nonsense holiday song to many people. But in reality it was a very special song with a very serious purpose. The song was written as a memory aid to encourage people's faith in Christ. It was filled with hidden codes and symbols! See if this list doesn't surprise you — and even help you remember the words!

On the first day of Christmas my *true love* gave to me...

True love=God the Father

A Partridge In A Pear Tree=Jesus Christ, the Son of God (He is represented as a partridge because a mother partridge will pretend to be injured to distract predators away from her helpless nestlings, thereby sacrificing her own life for those of her children)

Two Turtledoves=the Old and New Testaments

Three French Hens=Faith, Hope, and Love

Four Calling Birds=the four gospels: Matthew, Mark, Luke, and John

Five Golden Rings=the first five books of the Old Testament (also called the "Pentateuch")

Six Geese A-Laying=the six days in which God created the world

Seven Swans A-Swimming=the seven gifts of the Holy Spirit

Eight Maids A-Milking=the eight Beatitudes found in Matthew's Gospel

Nine Ladies Dancing=the nine fruit of the Holy Spirit

 Ten Lords A-Leaping=the Ten Commandments

 Eleven Pipers Piping=the eleven faithful apostles

 Twelve Drummers Drumming=the twelve elements of faith found in the Apostle's Creed

The Christmas Story

Of course, no Christmas party would be complete without the reading of the story of the birth of Jesus! So, be sure to

have a Bible on hand and plan to read aloud chapters one and two of the book of Matthew and/or chapters one and two of the book of Luke.

For to us a child is born,
to us a son is given,
and the government will be on his
shoulders.

And he will be called Wonderful Counselor,
Mighty God, Everlasting Father,
Prince of Peace.
Of the increase of his government and
peace there will be no end.
He will reign on David's throne
and over his kingdom,
establishing and upholding it
with justice and righteousness
from that time on and forever.

The zeal of the LORD Almighty
will accomplish this.

ISAIAH 9:6-7

Prayer Time

You may want to include a prayer time to close the evening. A brief time of prayer can be a wonderful way to quiet your spirits as the festivities wind down. Keeping things simple and low-key will make everyone comfortable, even those unfamiliar with religious language and customs. One way to do this is to gather everyone in a circle before you say goodnight and — as the hostess — begin by telling everyone what you are most grateful for this particular Christmas. One by one, each girl can name something for which she is especially grateful, and on it goes. When it comes back to you, end with a prayer of thanksgiving. You'll likely want to hug your friends and wish everyone a very merry Christmas. What a lovely way to end a fun and memorable Victorian party!

Don't Forget Clean Up!

Your party has been delightful. The guests have all enjoyed themselves. And now everyone has gone home. But wait! The Victorian hostess has one more important duty—cleaning up. Obviously, most of us don't have maids or servants to clean up for us as the Dinsmore family did. But the spirit of the party is incomplete without the spirit of service. Just as you dressed up and made your home beautiful, now you need to put everything back in its place and honor your home and your family who lives there. Don't be surprised if one or more of your

closer friends offers to help you with this task in advance. It's up to you to decide if you want them to stay "after" or not. It can actually be a lot of fun and makes the time fly by!

Follow-up

As an unusually kind gesture of friendship and love, consider sending thank you notes to the guests who attended your party. Since normally it is the other way around, with the guest sending a thank you to the hostess, your note will come as a wonderful surprise to your guests and will be an additional blessing to them. Use your thank you note not only to thank them for coming to the party, but also to tell them why their friendship is truly a special gift to you. This simple expression of your love and appreciation of them will probably mean

more to them than you will ever know. It may even be a letter that your friend cherishes forever.

A Final Word–
God's Free Gift to You:
The Gift of Salvation

When it comes to Christmas, there is one thing that matters most of all — Jesus Christ, the Savior of mankind! If you do not yet know Jesus personally, take the opportunity this season to listen to the teachings about Him and to investigate for yourself the story of the One who people throughout the world for the past 2,000 years have acknowledged as their Beloved Lord and God.

Jesus Christ, who was born in a manger in Bethlehem long, long ago, is alive and living today. Men and women, children and adults, young and old, rich and poor, people of all races and all nations, worship Him and follow Him. Decade after decade, century after century, and millennium after millennium, faith in Jesus Christ lives on. Why? Because Jesus Christ is who He said He was. He was not just a man or a great teacher. He was God in human flesh, sent to earth to redeem the sin and wickedness of all mankind.

You might not have committed "big" sins like murder, but at times you have probably committed lots of "little" sins, like being mean, selfish, disobedient, impatient, untruthful, ungrateful, unkind, or other things that are wrong in God's eyes. It is God, not man, who determines what is right and what is wrong. He alone sets the standards, and everything that falls short of God's standards is sin. Unfortunately, sin is what separates us from having a close relationship with God, for He is perfect and holy — completely pure and without sin. No amount of doing good deeds can ever erase your sins, and unless you are as perfect as God is, you cannot get into heaven or get close to Him.

Why does this matter? It matters because the God of the whole universe, the One who created heaven and earth and everything in them, created YOU! He made you just the way you are, and *He created you to have a relationship with Him.* Do you know that He loves you more than words can possibly express? God longs to show you how much He loves you. He wants to confide in you and tell you the secrets of His heart. He wants you to share the details of your life with Him, because He cares about you.

How can I have a relationship with God when I am such a sinner, you might ask. God Himself provided the solution. He loves you so much that He arranged for Jesus Christ, the perfect, sinless Son of God, to come to earth as a human being and be nailed to a Cross and die a horrible, painful death in order to pay the penalty for all of your sins and the sins of people everywhere. In doing this, God was giving you a free gift - the gift of forgiveness of your sins and eternal life with Him. What an awesome gift! It is a gift that no one can earn or buy. Although it cost God a great price, the death of His beloved Son, for you it is really and truly free. All you have to do is accept the gift.

If you want to have a personal relationship with God, you can have one right now, no matter how young or old you are. All you have to do is to accept the gift of Jesus Christ's death on the Cross for your sins and believe in Him with all your heart. If you invite Him to, He will send His Holy Spirit to live inside your heart. You will never be separated from Him again. We call this "becoming a Christian" and "being saved" because you are saved from the penalty of death and eternal separation from God.

If you want to become a Christian and be saved, it is as simple as saying a prayer to God. You can say it in your own words, or you can pray the following simple prayer, either alone or with another Christian:

Dear Heavenly Father,
I know that I am a sinner and have often done things that are wrong. I am sorry for my sins and I pray that you will forgive me for them. I accept the free gift of Jesus' death on the Cross in my place. I believe that Jesus died for my sins and was raised from the dead. I invite you, Father, Son and Holy Spirit, to come live inside my heart and change me for the better. I give my life to you right now, and I ask that from this day forth, you would help me to follow you, to love you more and more, and to get to know you better. Amen.

If you prayed to accept Jesus, *congratulations and welcome to the family of God!* Now you can look forward to a wonderful relationship with the Living God! Your sins have been washed away and you have been "born-again." (The first time you were born physically; this time you were born spiritually. Write down today's date, for it is your spiritual birthday and you will want to remember it!)

❧

Here are some things you should do next:

1) Tell someone else (preferably another Christian) about the commitment you just made to the Lord. If that someone else is not your parent, then you should also tell your mother or father (or your guardian). If he or she is not a Christian, then you should show them the previous section called "A Final Word" and have them read it too. It will help them understand the commitment you have made and why you made it.

2) Talk to God in prayer. You can speak to Him openly and honestly, at any time of the day or night, as often as you want. Pray for yourself as well as for other people. Tell God what is on your heart and

mind. Ask Him for wisdom and guidance when you need it. He loves you and is interested in your needs, your desires and the details of your life! Learn to share your life with Him. Be quick to ask for God's forgiveness when you do sin. And take time regularly to thank Him for His many blessings.

3) Get your own copy of the Holy Bible, the Word of God, in a translation that you can understand. Read from it every day. (A good place to start is the book of John.) Study the Scriptures and memorize your favorite verses. Expect God to speak to you through His Word.

4) Find a church that teaches the Bible and attend it regularly. Get involved in a Bible study group.

5) Seek out other Christians in your school or at your job or in other places and develop new friendships.

6) Tell others about your love for the Lord.

7) Guard your heart and do not let other people or other things steal your faith in and love for God.

8) Enjoy your relationship with your new best friend!

Bible Verses About Salvation

"For God so loved the world that He gave His one and only Son, that whoever believes in Him shall not perish but have eternal life." JOHN 3:16

"For Christ died for sins once for all, the righteous for the unrighteous, to bring you to God." 1 PETER 3:18

"For the wages of sin is death, but the gift of God is eternal life in Christ Jesus our Lord." ROMANS 6:23

"For all have sinned and fall short of the glory of God." ROMANS 3:23

"But God demonstrates His own love for us in this: While we were still sinners, Christ died for us." ROMANS 5:8

"For it is by grace you have been saved, through faith — and this not from yourselves, it is the gift of God — not by works, so that no one can boast." EPHESIANS 2:8-9

"If you confess with your mouth, 'Jesus is Lord,' and believe in your heart that God raised Him from the dead, you will be saved." ROMANS 10:9

A Christmas Blessing

We hope you have learned a lot about how to plan, prepare and host a successful, old-fashioned Christmas party, and that through this book you have also discovered the joy of giving your time and energy so that others might have pleasure. You may be a modern girl. But if you've enjoyed Elsie's Christmas Party, you are an old-fashioned girl at heart. And it is our prayer that this experience is just the beginning of your celebrating with friends and family in the gracious traditions of the Victorian era and lavishing love on others.

May the spirit of Christmas
Shine in your hearts.
May the love of God
Be seen in your lives.
And may the Blessed Christ Child
Come to dwell in your hearts.
And bring you love, joy, and peace
At this holy Christmas time.

Check out
www.elsie-dinsmore.com!

 Get news about Elsie

 Find out more about the 19th century world Elsie lives in

 Learn how to have a life of faith like Elsie's

 Learn about how Elsie overcomes the difficulties we all face in life

Find out about Elsie products

and more!

Elsie Dinsmore: A Life of Faith
"It's Like Having a Best Friend From Another Time"

Collect All of Our Elsie Dinsmore Books and Companion Products!

Elsie Dinsmore: A Life of Faith

Book One – Elsie's Endless Wait   ISBN 1-928749-01-1

Book Two – Elsie's Impossible Choice   ISBN 1-928749-02-X

Book Three – Elsie's New Life   ISBN 1-928749-03-8

Book Four – Elsie's Stolen Heart   ISBN 1-928749-04-6

Book Five – Elsie's True Love   ISBN 1-928749-05-4

Book Six – Elsie's Troubled Times   ISBN 1-928749-06-2

Watch for these upcoming Spring 2001 titles:

Elsie's Daily Diary

Elsie's Life Lessons, Volume 1

Book Seven – Elsie's Tender Mercies

Book Eight – Elsie's Great Hope